THE OASIS OF LIFE

───────⋅⋅───────

By

MATTHEW NEWELL

Copyright © Matthew Newell 2019
This book is sold subject to the condition that it shall not, by way of trade or otherwise, be lent, resold, hired out, or otherwise circulated without the publisher's prior consent in any form of binding or cover other than that in which it is published and without a similar condition including this condition being imposed on the subsequent publisher.
The moral right of Matthew Newell has been asserted.
www.matthewnewell.co.uk
ISBN: 9781072711506

DEDICATION

To my followers and my fans from all over the world.

Thank you for enjoying the ride and for your kind words.

To David and Joyce,
no longer here but always in my thoughts.

ACKNOWLEDGEMENTS

To the publishing team for their support and knowledge of making all this possible.

CONTENTS

1 A FIEND IN NEED 1
2 RESURRECTOR 15
3 THE BLACK LOTUS 28
4 EARTHEN CASKET 35
5 EXHUMED 42
6 LEUKOCYTES 51
7 WILDFIRE 55
8 HEARSEMAN OF THE APOCALYPSE 62
9 ISLAND RETREAT 69
10 PENNANCE 74
11 QUIETUS 80
12 CELESTIAL BURIAL 89
13 AVENGING ANGEL 96
14 GLASS HALF EMPTY 100
15 COLD SHOULDER 104
16 THE ONLOOKER 109
17 DEADWEIGHT 116
18 BRAIN FREEZE 123
19 NIGHT TERRORS 126
20 ADORCISM 135
21 MEMORY RETRIEVAL 141
22 CLEARWELL 146
23 DEPLETING CELLS 154
24 ENGRAM 161
25 THE OASIS OF LIFE 168
26 WHERE THERE'S A WILL 177
27 LOVING TRIBUTE 189
28 PARADISE LOST 194
29 CODA 198
ABOUT THE AUTHOR 203

This is a work of fiction. Names, characters, businesses, organizations, places, events and incidents either are the product of the author's imagination or are used fictitiously. Any resemblance to actual persons, living or dead, events, or locales is entirely coincidental.

1

A FIEND IN NEED

The widow, Petra Palmer, rested against her dusty and grease-caked worktop, lost deep in thought in her small but modest kitchen.

Pots and pans half filled with stagnant water piled high in the sunken sink beside her. But keeping on top of household chores was the last thing on her mind, as she stood there in her dreamlike state.

Her cell phone vibrated noisily into life and begun to violently shake across the dusty surface of the matt black worktop, leaving a jagged path. It sifted through the thick powder in its wake, making its way across to the recess of the stainless-steel sink that was coated in a milky white film.

Not giving the phone a single glance, Petra replayed past events over and over in her mind as if she was trying to make sense of what had happened to lead her up to this point in time.

Eight years ago, can that length of time really had passed so quick in a blink of an eye? she thought, as her eyes welled up to the pain of her late husband Stanley Palmer's passing.

Today was the anniversary of his death, but now only a cold, empty void remained in her heart where warmth and love once overflowed in abundance for him.

To make matters worse, it was hard to disguise her sunken, solemn mood which echoed that of the pouring rain that battered the kitchen window from outside, when she should still be celebrating her son Nathan's eighth birthday, which was only two days past.

Leaning against the worktop, she twirled within her left hand strands of her matted hair that had now weathered grey and had lost all sheen and radiance, draping unkempt about her shoulders.

In her right hand, she mindlessly toyed with a crystal glass pendant that hung from a silver chain around her neck, that had infused in its centre a striking depiction of a lone daisy. The pendant was cold but soothing to the touch as she tried to focus her mind.

The last time Petra had seen Stan alive was when he had visited her and baby Nathan in hospital, which had been a very joyous occasion.

The journey up until that moment had been tainted with much pain and suffering, but the birth of Nathan had swept all the anguish away and had made Petra and Stan closer.

Appreciating the bond of their increasing family, as they had two daughters already, a son was what Petra knew was needed to fulfil their lives more.

But Petra knew her husband only too well and on that same night, she had sensed Stan was harbouring a very dark secret, that unfortunately he would take to his grave as he left the ward and their lives forever.

Stanley Palmer had reoccurring health issues, with a brain tumour that had put him into a coma a couple of years earlier from a dreadful accident by the Mala Sort river close to where they lived.

He had endured his fight and awoken from his agonising sleep, but was never the same man he used to be. For although his recovery thereafter was good, Petra knew that the path to wellness was beset with relapses that Stan was trying his best to hide from her.

As a practicing Neurosurgeon, Petra knew only too well the battles that would lay ahead for the both of them.

But any slight pressure and concerned nagging she gave him would be tough for her husband, she knew this, as he was a proud man that liked to take on the world in his own way and not have to let his family suffer for him.

Eventually, on that cold and bleak night, he had exited the building and had taken a walk down to the Mala Sort river again. The destination was the last journey he would have taken when his brain had finally shut down.

Petra bit her bottom lip in frustration for her foolishness for not seeing the signs earlier. *If only things had gone better between their break down in conversation, then maybe Stan would still be here now.*

Her pregnancy with Nathan had zapped her of energy. Along with a hard labour, she almost died as a result of preeclampsia whilst they had been on holiday.

She and Nathan had survived that turmoil, so she found it hard to believe that Stan could give up so easily.

How futile life could truly be, she thought.

The bittersweet taste of the syrupy blood trickled down her throat, leaving a metallic tang behind as she recounted that later that night, and some hours later, she had an unexpected visit from the on-duty nurse in tow, with two police officers looking very timid and bearing grave news.

Petra had been happily breastfeeding Nathan when they came hurrying in and had to quickly snatch Nathan's mouth from her breast in haste to cover up her modesty.

The news of her late husband's demise still echoed loudly in her thoughts as the shocking event plagued her soul.

She was told there and then, with trepidation from the officers, that Stan must have had an accident, for there seemed no foul play was at work.

A jogger had been out running alongside the frosty banks of the river when he had spotted Stan's body face down in the centre of the iced-over stretch of water, frozen in time, on what would be the coldest night on record.

Oh, how she missed him, she never wanted him to go that way. *He must have been so lonely out there all by himself.*

Everything that had come after, from the housekeeping, to balancing work and raising Nathan had been numb and agonising.

It was at times like these today that she wished her dad Nathaniel was here to hug her. He, however, had long since passed away and now only his shortened name belonging to her son remained. At least her and Stan had agreed on their son's name on that occasion, for she knew he could be difficult at times to agree to anything.

At least Petra still had two daughters to support her, even though her youngest Sally had a family of her own and Anastasia was trying for one with her husband. They both had busy work lives to attend to, but were more than willing to lend support. They even made the effort to babysit every so often.

Fishing out her now silent, soggy phone from the sink, Petra dried the screen on her sweater and swiped to unlock it, looking at the name of the missed call. It was from Dustin, who was a close friend of the family, and who had once upon a time dated Stan's boss Natasha who also had been a rock to her in those early days of grief.

But Natasha and Dustin's relationship never lasted, for reasons still unknown to Petra to this day.

Like all good things, Petra figured, everything must come to an end one day. Death in its many forms would always break up a party.

She wondered if afterlife truly existed and, if it did, would it heal her broken heart when she was finally reunited with her soulmate? She prayed that it would.

Putting the phone to standby, Petra returned it to the worktop and reached for her preferred brand of cigarette that was half smouldering in the ashtray that she had absentmindedly forgotten was there.

She brought the butt up to her lips to take a drag, but the pain of the hot nicotine stung her open wound and forced her to throw it into one of the pots of water with a hiss.

Glancing to the outside rain that lashed the window, Petra brought up her sweater sleeve and wiped the fresh blood away.

Condensation built up on the inside of the glass of the window and slightly obscured the haggard reflection of herself within.

Trickles of water bubbled through the rotten, framed window as another stale thought came into her mind.

The day of Stan's funeral had been chaotic and was steeped in so much negativity that Petra had prayed that the long day would just end or the cemetery would just swallow her whole.

From the hearse getting a puncture en-route, to the sodden coffin being dropped just shy of the catafalque, that dark day was a nightmare of horrors.

Nathan's demands and constant crying had been the only real thing that made sense to her in the calamity that ensued, for inside herself she was screaming at the top of her lungs, *Why God is this happening to me?!*

Time, as it always did, moved on, but Petra's scars were still on show for all to see. Dustin had grown very close to her and Nathan over time, as she and Natasha had grown further apart.

Petra guessed that it must have been Dustin's guilt that made him hang around, as he happened to work in the funeral industry as a regular hearse driver, who in possession of Stan's body on his funeral that day, seemed to carry the brunt of all the things that had gone wrong.

The funeral had been delayed by twenty minutes as the hearse had a wheel blow out and Dustin and the conductor had to quickly change it at the side of the road.

Dustin's knuckles were bleeding profusely by the time a fresh tyre was mounted on, as his hands had scraped the surface of the road in removing the dud tyre off.

To top it off for Dustin, when he was pall-bearer for Stan's coffin, he twisted his ankle whilst carrying the load into the crematorium and fell to the floor in agony. The coffin slid away from the other three pall-bearers and crashed into his ribs, sending out a large resounding echo around the chapel as the heavy coffin then hit the marbled floor, muffling his screams. The looks of the shocked congregation still haunted Petra today.

It was like Stan had it in for him, Dustin had guessed, but never shared his thoughts with Petra. He did, after all, kill Stan's pet cat and was there just before Stan died, when he had confronted him about the death of his own father whom he blamed on Stan when Stan was but a child.

Dustin's dad had been the minibus driver that ferried Stan and a few of his fellow pupils to and from school. But one day, Stan had caused Dustin's dad to veer off road, that resulted in the bus careering down the gorge and out into the rapids of the Mala

Sort river, where all but one soul had perished... Stan had been the only survivor.

So, there was Dustin now getting his comeuppance as he looked to his partner Natasha, who was attending and seated nearby in the crematorium and who was still very much his partner at the time, pleading for her to help.

She raced over to join all those already involved in the struggle, clumsily trying their best to get the coffin to its resting place, which was now worse for wear with the flower spray now higgledy-piggledy and askew on the top of the casket. Dustin was amazed that he still had a job after that day.

Stan, whose soul had not long said farewell to the world, had indeed been orchestrating the enfolding events from beyond the grave, but his energy was not quite yet harnessed to do harm to Dustin, as he had envisioned.

It was like he was on the wrong side of the door, for death was just the beginning of a soul's journey.

Eight years later, and to Stan's great comfort whilst he bided his time in the Astral plain that existed between Earth and paradise, something wonderful had happened. Petra had turned Stan's ashes into a daisy pendant that she now wore around her neck that also served her, without knowing it, to be a tether that linked the world he found himself in to our world.

Stan was pleased, as the pendant acted as a Talisman that would ward of evil and allow him to reach out in subtle ways to connect to the Earth and his wife, including that of the advances from Dustin towards her.

As for the rest of Stan's ashes, they were encased in an urn to be buried later, waiting to be transferred into three fireworks that Stan had requested in his will, to be shot up into the sky above the town where he grew up.

It was Dustin's confession of his guilt that tore his relationship with Natasha apart many months later as he implored her forgiveness and to keep his dark secret.

Which she did to the present day, but the forgiveness Dustin sought would never, ever come, in the end they went their heartbroken, separate ways.

A key struck the lock to the front door and rattled in the casing, bringing Petra back to reality from her dark past.

'In you go then, Nathan, and make sure you take your raincoat straight off to hang up and whilst you're at it, get out of those wet shoes before you leave the hallway to go see mummy,' a cheery voice said from behind a large brown umbrella that was being shaken free of water.

Petra tucked the pendant back into her yellow sweater, wiped her tears and stepped out into the hallway.

On seeing Nathan bounding towards her, she bent down and scooped him up into her arms before nuzzling his neck which caused him to giggle.

'How's my favourite boy?' she asked, looking over his shoulder to the figure stepping through the threshold to hang up the now closed umbrella.

'He was as good as gold. I think he enjoys being

with his uncle Dustin as much as I enjoy looking after him,' the figure replied in answer to her open question.

The pendant beneath Petra's thick sweater slightly shimmered.

Nathan uncoupled from his mum then darted off around her to switch on the television in the adjacent living room.

Dustin removed his damp coat and slung it casually over the stairs bannister and approached Petra to give her a big hug and a kiss to the cheek.

An overhanging light bulb popped in its fitting and showered Dustin in fine glass dust.

'Damn! I keep telling you that you could do with a handyman around here. I'm more than happy to help,' Dustin said, noticing Petra's dried, streaked cheeks.

Petra lightly pushed him away, 'Thank you, Dusty,' she said, turning away from him to go retrieve a cigarette.

'You going to be alright? Or would you like some company tonight?' Dustin said, following her into the kitchen.

A photo of Stan, Petra and their two daughters encased in its frame fell off the wall in the living room, alerting Nathan who went to pick it up.

Petra, startled by the noise it made when it hit the floor, turned to Dustin, 'I don't think it's a good idea today, Dusty. You know what day it is. I think it's best that I spend some time alone with Nathan today. But thank you for taking him out for a while. I do appreciate it,' she said, lighting up and ignoring the pain from her lip.

Dustin threw open his hands, 'Sure, no problem. You know I'm happy to help you out any time,' he said, looking into her hollow eyes.

Petra went to walk into the living room to take the photo from Nathan when Dustin grabbed her shoulder, 'Are we still on for me moving into the guest room? Because I'm all packed and ready to move in. Then I can pay my way and get this house back to some kind of normality,' he said, looking at the unwashed dishes and rotten window frame that had painted splinters of wood peeling away.

'Soon,' Petra said, then added 'I just need a little more time to adjust.'

'Okay, that's fine. Just give me a call when you're ready,' he said, retreating back down the hallway to retrieve his coat.

Petra gave him a faint smile just as a gust of wind blew the front door wide open, almost knocking Dustin into the wall and blowing the ash clean off her cigarette.

'Don't leave it too long,' he said gesturing to the door, 'It's not just the house that needs some TLC,' he added, throwing on his coat and blowing her a kiss.

With that he stepped back out into the downpour once more, but just as he was about to close the door behind him, another gust of wind slammed the door shut in his face.

The daisy pendant around Petra's neck radiated a gentle warmth as if it was content once more.

Petra discarded the extinguished cigarette and turned her attention back to Nathan, who had suddenly seemed like he had seen a ghost as he stood there shaking, looking as white as a sheet, still holding the photo frame and talking to himself.

'Well I don't like him. Well and I don't like you either, you're mean and horrible to me,' Nathan said, quivering.

Petra approached him and knelt down to give him a hug, she removed the photo from his hands, tears welling up again.

'Oh, Nathan my poor son,' Petra said, pulling him in tighter, 'I thought those days of your imaginary friend being around had long since gone.'

'Guess again bitch!' Nathan screamed in a deeper pitch than his own normal voice, as he struggled out of her grasp.

Petra, taken aback and in shock, slapped his face. 'Don't you dare talk to mummy like that!' she roared.

Then all of a sudden, the glass in the frame shattered into a thousand pieces, exploding over their heads. Petra reasoned the stress and tightness with which she held it had caused it to shatter. She screamed out loud in surprise as Nathan then suddenly turned menacingly to her, 'Tough luck. Nathan's not here right now. I am and I'm getting stronger all the time, I am going to get what I want, and no one will challenge me, especially him,' he said, pointing to Stan in the photo of the now glassless frame.

The pendant beat hard against Petra's chest and gave her an inner strength she didn't know she had. Petra threw her arms around Nathan and brought him in close to a warm embrace.

A mother's love and the unseen force of the pendant connected with the dark soul that was within Nathan, making the child scream out as if in pain, before he collapsed defeated in her arms. 'I'm sorry mummy, I won't let him hurt you again,' he said, sobbing, whilst burrowing his head into hers.

Later that night, having tucked a miserable Nathan into his bed, Petra returned downstairs and fixed herself a stiff drink. It was a dusty bottle of half-drunk whiskey that had belonged to Stan, from a long time ago.

As she stood over the bin, cradling the glass of whiskey, Petra looked at the remnants of the broken glass and frame with sadness in her eyes.

She gulped down a large shot and retrieved the now crumpled photo from her jeans pocket, to look longingly at the image of loving memories from long ago.

'Why did you have to leave me Stan?' she whispered, but she knew no answer would come.

She made her way to the back door that overlooked a messy garden, overgrown with wild flowers intermingled with weeds, as she gazed up into the night sky.

She knew Nathan was unlike any other child of his age. He often spoke of his other mummy and of some past life that Petra could not understand, but she had never got around to taking him to a physician.

It was like Nathan harboured an ancient soul that had gotten itself attached to her son.

The imaginary friend of his had now manifested

again but this time it was more malevolent than previous past encounters. As Nathan got older, so the other persona got stronger.

It called itself Will. Could it be the same Will that sacrificed himself to save Stan from the minibus wreckage all those years ago? Was it just a coincidence? Had she imagined Nathan saying the name? Or was it a name he heard in passing? Petra thought long and hard, but in the end, she finished her drink and decided to put it down to an overactive imagination of a sensitive son who had no father to idolise, even though he was still too young to fully understand.

Petra popped her empty glass into the cluttered sink, strode over to the wooden urn, gave it a gentle kiss and retired to bed.

She hoped Nathan would outgrow this difficult time and mature into a wonderful man one day, just like his dad Stanley had been.

Another long night lay ahead, with a large, cold bed waiting, the only warmth from the pit of her stomach slowly draining away as the whisky subsided.

2

RESURRECTOR

Making sure his sister Anastasia and her husband were sound asleep, Nathan Palmer, now sixteen years old, gently closed their bedroom door and hoisted the satchel over his shoulder, containing three fireworks, each loaded with a teaspoon of his father's ashes sealed in each of them, prepped and ready for tomorrow's launch with his family. But he had other ideas.

Most of his father's ashes had been buried already and were now marked by a moderate headstone up in the old cemetery.

He was not aware of the traces of his late dad's ashes that were infused with his mum's daisy glass pendant that she wore around her neck.

His sister, for the last couple of years, had been kind enough to put him up in a spare room that was originally going to be a nursery, but she and her husband were never able to conceive. They felt great love towards Nathan even though he was a nightmare to live with. But they would never see him out on the street, so were happy to convert it to his lodgings.

The wayward young Nathan was forever getting in

to some kind of trouble or other and in the end, his stepfather had intervened against Petra's wishes and finally kicked him out of the family home.

Nathan was thankful for his sister to accommodate him.

Creeping downstairs, Nathan eyed the car keys sitting in the drop-off point on the hallway dresser and slipped them into his pocket, before steeling out into the darkness of the bleak, wet and miserable night.

He approached the dark blue sedan, clicked the door to unlock on the fob and opened the door.

Twenty minutes later, he had picked up two of his equally troubled friends and was now recklessly steering the stolen vehicle down the puddle-strewn streets, avoiding the sparse traffic as he veered in and out of any cars that crossed his path.

Turning up the Bass on the volume of the in-car stereo, Nathan narrowly avoided bouncing up a kerb and wiping out a middle-aged couple, huddled under a brightly coloured golfing umbrella, as they walked silently hand in hand along a desolate pavement.

Nathan looked into the vibrating rear-view mirror to his friend Cade who was swigging from a can of beer in the back seat, 'Cade, pull down the back and look for anything interesting in the boot.'

'Okay sure. What am I looking for?' Cade said, tossing the now empty can out of the window.

'I don't know, anything useful,' Nathan said, as a headlight from a trailing car lit up his darkened, wicked eyes in the mirror.

'Haiden, pass me a beer and roll me a snout,'

Nathan said, presenting the passenger to his left a tobacco tin from his black bomber jacket pocket.

'Lots of crap back here,' Cade shouted over his shoulder, squirming around half buried in the boot, flashing the light from his mobile phone around its darkened interior.

Increasing the speed and hurtling around a bend into a black-mirrored puddle, Nathan smirked as the car aquaplaned through, showering a homeless man hankered down for the night in a shop porch.

'Well, let's see what we've got then,' he said.

Cade returned from the black void wielding a pair of old wellingtons and a set of jump leads, 'Like I said, nothing of interest... wait a minute though, what's this down in the footwell?' he said, discarding the items in hand.

Reaching down he pulled on a long-handled tool and grunted as he pulled it up onto his lap to study it, 'Got ourselves a sledgehammer, is this useful enough?' he beamed.

Nathan grinded the gears as he shifted up, 'Yeah, I was hoping that was still in here, noticed it a few days ago. Might come in handy, Cade. Haiden, you rolled that cigarette yet?'

Haiden had just finished running the paper's glue across his tongue, 'Hmm, here you go,' he said, rolling it closed and running his fingers around it to seal it up properly.

Nathan snatched it from his hands and stuck it behind his ear; 'Light?'

Haiden fished a lighter from his jeans pocket and

passed it along with the tobacco tin to Nathan. 'So, where we going anyway?' he said, proceeding to reach down to retrieve a cold can of beer from between his feet.

'I think we should smash up some bus stops or parked cars,' Cade said, wielding the sledgehammer over his shoulder and pretending to bring it down onto Haiden's head.

Haiden grabbed a hold of the heavy steel end, 'Leave it out, Cade you idiot, I'm not getting in to trouble again with you,' he said, trying to wrestle the hammer from Cade's grasp.

'Don't worry, I've got something better to do with that,' Nathan said, taking the sledge hammer off the both of them and laying it across his lap.

Eventually, the blue sedan with the louts sped passed the main road containing a row of various shops and travel agents and made their way to a church sitting grand on a crest of a hill.

They were now driving on the wrong side of the road and swerved at the last minute to avoid an oncoming van containing two undertakers that were on a coroner's call out.

Nathan, with only malice on his mind, didn't even recognise one of the occupants of the vehicle they just missed, as being Dustin, who had definitely recognised his stepson driving his sister's stolen car.

'Seriously! He will be the death of me,' Dustin said, hitting the brakes, sending the wheeled trolley in the van's rear-hold slamming into the dividing steel wall behind their seats.

'Too bloody right,' the passenger, Blake, said, leaning out of his window into the downpour of the night. 'See you real soon, morons,' he shouted after them.

'Oh, we will see them before they see us,' Dustin said, slamming the van into a three-point turn.

'You what, what are you doing Dusty?' Blake said, reeling his head back in from the sleet that battered his face.

'Going after them. That boy who was driving the car... that's my stepson, Nate. When I catch up with him, I'll throttle him,' Dustin said, forcing the steering wheel hard right and lurching the van forward, kicking up loose gravel between its tyre treads.

'What about our call out? We've got less than thirty minutes now to get to the scene to collect our deceased, we can't risk losing the contract. I for one don't want to lose my job over it,' Blake exclaimed, checking his seatbelt was still securely fastened.

'Screw it, I'm not letting this one slide. Nate has put my wife Petra through enough over the years as it is,' Dustin replied.

Fast approaching the green traffic lights that were up ahead, Dustin noticed the lad's car disappearing down the lane that split between the church and the vicarage.

The neon green reflection of the light rippled across the surface of the oily puddle as the van's wheels cut through its wake.

'You're well over the speed limit, Dusty, the tracker is going to flag this up in the morning. Slow down, will you? I don't want to end up in a wagon like this one just yet,' Blake said, anxiously gripping both his knees hard as they passed through the lights.

Dustin didn't hear him, he was too focused on catching up with the lead vehicle and had misjudged the corner of the narrow lane, as a rogue branch collided with the wing mirror and yanked it clean off.

'Whoa! Now we're going to have to pay for the damage too!' Blake cried, wishing he had been given a different on-call partner.

'Just shut up, Blake!' Dustin said, with anger boiling over.

By the time the removal vehicle had caught up to the sedan, the occupants had long abandoned it and were well on their way, picking a path through the church cemetery.

Nathan was dragging the sledgehammer behind him with his satchel around his neck, the fireworks jostled around the hold as they poked out from beneath the flap. Haiden and Cade were vaulting over headstones to catch him up.

'We're not going to smash the church up, are we?' Haiden asked nervously.

'No! I'm going to find my dad, the man who ruined my life,' Nathan said, rounding the corner of the church.

Cade shouted after him, 'I thought he was…you know… dead?' He said, through hushed tones.

'He is. But a voice inside is telling me I've got to see him, I can't explain it though, so just go with it alright?' Nathan said, sounding impatient, as he found the grave's marker and came to an abrupt halt.

Nathan's friends exchanged troubled looks. 'He's not thinking of digging up his dad, is he?' Haiden said on the quiet to Cade.

'I bloody well hope not,' Cade hissed.

'What's more worrying is the voice inside his head that he complains about all the time, I hope he's not skitzo,' Haiden added, starting to freak out with the eerie silence that had now descended upon them.

Gathering around the weathered headstone, Haiden and Cade eyed Nathan cautiously, as they slowed down upon catching him up.

'So, err, what are we going to do now?' Cade said, yanking a full can of beer from his oversized pockets to drink from, for Dutch courage.

Not getting an immediate answer, Cade pulled off the can's ring pull and slurped from it, fearful of the answer that he was sure to hear, that he knew would eventually come.

Nathan pulled the rolled-up cigarette from his ear and lit it up, 'Now, I'll tell you what. Now I'm going to obliterate this headstone,' he said, taking a slow burning puff.

He took another few pulls on the cigarette and removed the satchel from his shoulder, casually dumping it on the floor. 'Grab a firework each from the bag and both of you split up, Haiden go stand over there,' he said, pointing to a nearby tree. 'Cade, you over there,' he added, pointing to a grave thirty yards to the left of Haiden. 'I'm going to put the last one in the ground just behind my dad's headstone, pointing directly at it. I want a triangle formation and I want them all pointed at my dad's headstone... GOT IT?' he demanded, taking his firework from the satchel and walking around to the rear of the black, marble headstone.

Cade and Haiden dutifully nodded, grabbed a firework obediently, then went to take up positions.

Once all fireworks were in position, Nathan walked back round to the front of the headstone and swung the hammer up over his shoulder and poised himself ready to strike down unto it with brute force.

'Once I've smashed this and gone to light my firework, then I want you both to set off yours... no matter what happens, understand?' he huffed, with the cigarette hanging from his lips.

Cade and Haiden nodded.

'I suggest you light them at the same time I do mine, you got it?' Nathan said, looking to each of them in turn, with a wild rage in his eyes.

The friends nodded again, then gave each other a puzzled look.

Nathan's hands felt cold and clammy as he gripped hard onto the sledgehammer. The rain flattened his blond spiky hair, causing the gel to run down his forehead.

With an almighty swing, the hammer hit the headstone and split it cleanly in two, just as a fork of lightning cracked the dark clouded sky, blotting out the noise of the impact.

Nathan fell to his knees and dropped the hammer beside him. 'Dad! Show yourself!' he said, fighting back the tears, then added 'William Last wants a word with you.'

Unseen to his friends, a mist began to ooze from the jagged remains of the split headstone, slowly swirling and taking shape into the form of a man...Nathan's dad...Stanley Palmer.

It was just at that instance when Dustin came storming in to view, with a fiery temper, from around the corner of the church, having left his partner inspecting the van's damage.

'Nate. What the hell do you think you're...' Dustin trailed off, seeing what Nathan had done. 'My god, boy, are you really that sick?' he said, grabbing Nathan from behind by both shoulders and hauling him to his feet.

Nathan spun around uncontrollably, lunged for the sledgehammer and swung it hard into Dustin's shoulder which made a large cracking sound as it splintered bone, shattering his step-father's scapula.

Dustin fell screaming in agony to the wet, mud-stricken ground.

'Your little Nate is no more, Dusty. I, William Last am here now and all shall answer to me.' the deep growl of Will bellowed.

The ghostly memory of Stanley Palmer, having now fully developed into a clearer image from the eerie mist, floated across to the now possessed Nathan.

'Will, you don't have to do this, please release my son before it's too late. You can both come through this unscathed. One way or another you cannot continue on this dark path,' the spectral image said, with an air of calm and grace.

Haiden and Cade, now in horror of seeing the pain inflicted on Nathan's step-dad, awkwardly glanced at one another, lit the fireworks laden with Stan's ashes and ran off petrified into the night.

William Last, now in control of Nathan's form, howled into the storm as he realised the fireworks were lit too soon, 'No! I'm not ready yet!' he screamed, slipping and sliding as he raced over to light his own firework.

Dustin pulled himself up, cradling his arm, and approached the ghost of Stan that he now saw before him. Disbelievingly and in shock he pleaded, 'Stan. Stanley, is that really you? I'm sorry, I'm so sorry for killing Heparin, your beloved cat… please forgive me,' he said, crying loudly with pain and regret.

But they were to be the last words that came out of his mouth.

The lit fireworks had burnt away the fuse and ignited the gunpowder, shooting across the cemetery in a hot fiery haze, hitting him with double force in an explosion of bangs and whizzes.

Dustin's screams penetrated the silent night, as he then went running blindly through the cemetery in flames, billowing smoke behind him with the rain sizzling off his burning body.

Will went to turn back when he realised what happened. The plan was to shoot the ashes of Stan at Stan's own ghost, that in turn would break Stan's astral link to this world.

Then Will could go unchecked and create an army

on Earth with no Stan from beyond the grave to stop him.

Sensing Will's intention of reaching the last remaining firework for reasons he did not yet comprehend, and still feeling great sadness for Dustin's demise behind him that smoldered in the night, for in the afterlife he had learned to forgive all injustices, Stan summoned with all his energy a calling of five angels to show themselves at his bequest.

Sure enough, and to Will's disgust, moments later, five spectral winged angels materialised in a circle around him.

Will lit the last firework with wet, shaking hands from the hot smouldering tip from his cigarette, swung the firework round and pointed it at the ghost of Stan.

The angels were too slow to close rank and their feeble efforts to protect Stan by sacrificing themselves were in vain as the rocket found its mark.

Stanley Palmer did not know the true intent of the fireworks purpose and that it could erase his one shot of stopping Will's world domination.

The ark of light with the holy, ashen remains of Stan exploded in a carousel of dancing colour, sending Stan's surprised spirit back once more to the astral plain from where he came.

William Last flashed a wicked grin to the advancing angels that had him now surrounded in a circle, 'You've no way of getting home now little birds and your power has no anchor here without Stan. I'm going to enjoy converting you to my cause. But first, I don't like the white of your feathers so I think I'm going to make them blood red as I clip them,' he said, bringing his hands up and uprooting all the headstones in the cemetery by an unseen telekinetic-like force which sent large clods of earth flying outwards around him.

A light came on from a window in the vicarage nearby, just as the angels looked around nervously at a darker cloud descending over them. A swirling torrent of heavy-set headstones circled overhead.

It was if a tornado had uprooted them and was now pulling them up, spinning into the heart of its funnel.

Yanking back the curtains, a chubby vicar peered out from the confines of his domain. What he saw unfolding before him was the work of the devil.

The words R.I.P engraved on some of the headstones now held greater meaning, as they targeted their prey from high above, before raining down with fire and brimstone with lethal force on the winged victims below.

The vicar's heart gave out. He clutched at his chest and fell away from the frame of the window.

Nathan Palmer's soul was now truly lost, as William's evil spirit took hold of his diminishing light entirely.

William Last had finally acquired power on Earth to wield an unimaginable, supernatural power.

Dustin lay motionless and quite dead, smoking in the ruined grounds of the cemetery.

Stanley Palmer was banished back to the afterlife with very little options left to prevent any further catastrophe's happening on Earth as he was tasked to do.

Petra Palmer, asleep in her lonely bed, held the softly humming pendant close to her chest, now a widow once more.

Any glimmer of faith and hope were fading fast, as the tulpa, William Last, an evil figment-made-flesh of Stan's once troubled mind, was resurrected to stake his claim on Earth.

For the outside world, it was as if a remote, freak hurricane was taking place.

The trapped Nathan Palmer, now a slave to his split personality, thought he was having a schizophrenic episode, as his alter ego laughed menacingly into the night.

3

THE BLACK LOTUS

Nestled deep within the confines of Nate's subconscious, floated an island that lay abandoned and overpopulated with decaying trees, starved of natural light. The island was surrounded on all sides by a raging torrent of sea. A sad reflection of his troubled state of mind. A place of limbo between our world and the next.

The island was in a transitional period, caught between the cusp of a wet Autumn and a long approaching icy winter.

Trees that covered the stretch of land mass reached out their twisted branches to the heavens, as if in agony and torment, as the last brown and withered leaves that had been clinging on to them for dear life were wrenched from the branches. The gusts steeling them away into the beseeching winds that whistled through the dying canopies.

Amid the battle of the elements and rooted firmly at the centre of the island, bathed in the only light that could penetrate the isle, in a small clearing, was a magnificent black structure that resembled a closed

Lotus flower that rose eight feet in stature with a circumference of around four feet, that sat in a basin of emerald green tinged water, laced with yellow soggy leaves.

On closer inspection, each giant petal of the Lotus were individually segmented feathers which overlapped one another, forming an impenetrable tightly woven and deadly bond.

Each feather was razor sharp to the touch and made from some other-worldly metal composite.

Inside the dark recess of the Lotus flower, which was in fact the crouched state of a dark angel, sat two figures who were engaged in a hushed conversation.

'You weren't to know the outcome would play out as it did,' stated one of the figures, whose face was up close to the other.

'But I should have expected it, I can't believe that I was blindsided by my own ill-judgement of the situation. Now I'm afraid we are all out of options. How could I have been so stupid, Ictus?' the second figure said, squirming in the fetal position that he lay.

Ictus, whose mighty wings which made up the Lotus design that was sheltering the two of them from the outside world, stretched within the makeshift cocoon and flexed one of the barbs of a feather to let a little light shine in from outside.

'Stan, like a Lotus flower we open with the light of the sun and close to the darkness of the night, ready to start the next day anew, a rebirth if you will. So, we will try again. I have every faith that we will succeed next time by learning from our lessons and trying something new and untested,' Ictus said, craning its withered ear to the outside wailing winds and the rustling of leaves.

'If Will unearths my remaining ashes and scatters them, then I will have no way of returning to Earth to prevent him spreading his evil upon the world and my son will be lost,' Stan said, squinting to the shaft of light.

'It will be worse than that, Stan. If Will scatters all your ashes on earth, it will have a detrimental effect here too. You WILL end up lost in limbo,' Ictus said, grabbing hold of Stan's shoulders and looking deep into his eyes.

'I can't let that happen, I mustn't, Ictus. My son, my family, the world, they are all relying on me, it's just they don't know it yet,' Stan said, rebuffing the shock factor of Ictus' statement.

'You are vulnerable whilst you are in spirit form on Earth just as you are vulnerable here, existing as a deep-planted memory within your son's mind, an interloper in a foreign land, but Will is vulnerable too. If we can...'

SNAP!

The sound of a branch braking in the outside wilderness alerted Ictus' fine sense of hearing.

The dark Angel brought a sharp taloned finger up to its lips and gave Stan a worrying look. 'Leukocytes, Stan, be still,' Ictus said, closing the light out from between the feathers, plunging them both once more into darkness.

'What are Leukocytes?' Stan whispered, straining to listen beyond the walls he was enclosed in.

'Shhh!' Ictus said, pushing a palm into a pool of water beneath them and releasing an object from its grasp into the depths.

'What are you doing?' Stan mouthed silently.

Ictus brought its free hand up in protest. 'Quiet.'

Time seemed to drag in the silent void for Stan, as he lay there curled up in a ball with his back pressed against the feather incisored wall. His thoughts were his only comfort in a dark cold tomb.

Eventually light seeped in once more as Ictus became less tense and then removed the wet hand from the pool.

'It is safe for now Stan, but I don't know for how long. Obviously, the pool beneath us is where your son was brought into being and where he passed from thought into matter on Earth as a conscious being. It is also why we were forced here in the first place, but look where that got us,' Ictus said, stroking its chin, 'with my protection, to allow you to converse back with Will on Earth by using the tether between here between our worlds, I was hoping I might read his thoughts at the source. It works in the same way that Petra's pendant does, to act as a receiver to Earth. What I have uncovered is not much to go on though, just a snippet of information I have gleaned I'm afraid, but he too will sense us.'

'What have you learned then, Ictus?' Stan said, pushing his fingers into the pool to try and get a reading himself.

Stan felt something like a smooth pebble nestled into the mud below the surface, but it was slimy and soft, he pulled his hand away in disgust and was about to mention it to Ictus when he was cut short. 'Pay attention, Stan.'

'When Will possessed your son's body, he inadvertently imprisoned Nate's soul somewhere here in this island of his mind. In doing so, he has made himself open to attack on Earth but any further travels there may seriously jeopardize all we wish to achieve,' Ictus said, letting his mind piece it all together.

'Well it is something to go on, I'll take the risk. So how can I get back to finish what I started?' Stan said, with fresh optimism and determination.

'Not so fast, Stan. Will has corrupted the five angels that were sent to aid your quest on Earth. Now having been defeated, they will be forced to do his bidding acting as *Dakini*.'

'What's a *Dakini*?'

'Subservient angels, Stan. Anyway, here in the Astral plain, they will be used to suppress Nate from hijacking his body back. Here they will serve their true purpose.'

'Which is?' Stan said, rubbing the cramp that had grown in his legs.

'To attack foreign bodies that have materialised in the host, as white cells are triggered to attack when one appears.'

'So, I'm the invading foreign body...' Stan added.

'...and they are the Leukocytes,' Ictus said, finishing off Stan's sentence.

'So, Will wishes to spread all my ashes to the four corners of the world to prevent my return and send me to purgatory here, by erasing my son's memory of me. Once I'm out of the equation he can potentially create an army on Earth, kill them all off and march his army right up to paradise in the Astral plain and overthrow us all,' Stan said, summing it all up.

'That's pretty much it, Stan,' Ictus said.

'Phew! Okay, so what's the play now then?' Stan half laughed, not at all surprised by the absurd revelation.

'Well we can't do anything on Earth right now as it's too risky for you, but there is plenty we can do from here. First we need a priest and above all we must avoid the Leukocytes at all costs, because if they catch you, it's over.'

Stan raised his eyebrows at Ictus then clapped his hands together dispersing the water between his palms. 'All right, let's do this,' he said, then added 'open up and let's get going, I've come a long way and I am more ready now than I ever was.'

Ictus started to unfurl its wings to bathe them in light when it suddenly stopped short.

'I'm afraid we can't go just yet, Stan.'

Stan, who had half stretched out to stand up, found himself looking around bewildered at the twisted trees around them, 'What is it Ictus?' he whispered, nervously, bobbing back down.

'I'm not sure yet Stan, I know it's been sixteen years since we were last here, and I appreciate that we had no choice but to wait this long to come, but Will has had equal time to prepare for our arrival as we have to plan a strike. He's up to something! To arrive here unimpeded and for you to fail on Earth, I thought it would be Will's last desperate move. I'm convinced now, however, that because of his arrogance, he would fully expect his plan to have worked and so would follow up an attack to eradicate you here and now.'

Another branch cracked in the near distance.

Ictus forced Stan down to his knees with urgency, 'The Leukocytes are coming Stan!'.

With that, Ictus clammed up quick, like a Venus fly trap that had just ensnared its pray, leaving Stan back in the dark and feeling more vulnerable and more worried than he had ever been in all the days he had been alive on earth.

4

EARTHEN CASKET

The doppelganger, William Last, snatched his satchel from the passenger seat of the removal van and kicked the door shut, before striding off to the edge of the precipice that overlooked the Mala Sort river.

Slinging the frayed satchel down into the weeds that clumped together at the ravines edge, the youthful Will, in the guise of the trapped Nate, sat down and swung his legs over the lip then pulled the bag onto his lap.

The midday sun hung listless in the cloudless sky and shone brightly through the trees and vegetation that ran across the South side of the river bank, obscuring the busy carriageway beyond.

Will unbuckled the bag and began rooting around inside, pushing a curved needle, a reel of bloody thread and a capped scalpel out of his way to retrieve from within its depths a sandwich wrapped in cling film which he began to slowly unwrap.

A dull repetitive banging on metal broke the silence behind him from the vicinity of the van.

Will fumbled in the dirt beside him and grabbed a small rock that he slung over his shoulder and walked to the parked vehicle, he hit it with a loud twang. 'Quiet, I've told you already that I will deal with you in due course,' he said, turning back to his whole meal sandwich with its piccalilli filling.

Eventually, the banging died down and Will finished eating his stolen meal, he scrunched up the wrapping and flicked it over the ravine, watching it tumble down the steep slope into the calm-flowing river below, where it then sailed off lazily downstream.

Reaching into the hold of the bag once more, but with both hands this time, he dragged a well weathered, pine casket out from its resting place and studied the mud-caked box in front of him, giving it a shake and turning it over and over, pondering his next move.

He traced a dirty thumb across the bevelled lid that was screwed down and took pleasure in scraping off clods of ground-in dirt that were stuck in the grooves.

'Such a peaceful place Stan, don't you think? Funny that a place of such beauty should hide a shared dark past such as ours,' he said, referring to the river below.

'Of course, I can now admire the tranquility of it all, which you had denied me for so long, and all whilst you slide further into oblivion,' Will said to himself, gloating, knowing that Stan was helpless and far away, imprisoned in a cell of his own doing. Dead but not forgotten.

Heat rose from the glossy black van behind him and the occupant in the hold began to create a racket again.

Will looked over his shoulder and just shook his head. 'You know Stan, for a minute there I really thought you had gotten the better of me, especially with Dustin showing up unannounced like he did and almost ruining everything. Ah poor old Dusty, or should I say poor step-father, taking the full force of the fireworks like he did.'

Will rubbed the dirt away from his thumb and forefinger.

'I've actually done you a favour there haven't I? Who would believe that the man that betrayed you, by killing your beloved cat, could worm his way into your wife's life just so easily as he did? Well I guess now he really did jump into your grave didn't he? I wonder what his lost soul is doing now?' Will chuckled.

'The best thing is though, those fireworks that killed Dusty were modified by me to give a little extra kick to proceedings, along with the traces of your ashes. So technically, you helped in bringing about his end,' Will added, placing the box to the side of him and standing up to stretch.

Will strode over to the rear of the van, pushed the button in at the release of the handle and pulled the door up with a whoosh.

Inside the removal vehicle was a hydraulic lift that had been raised half-way up and was separated on both levels by two metal flaps, one on the top layer and one on the bottom.

Will peered in over the top flap on the upper deck, 'If you stay quiet just a little longer then I promise you that I will leave the door up, okay?' he said, before yanking down the flap on the bottom tier and pulling the sledgehammer out that he had stowed in there earlier the night before.

The occupant whimpered in obedience.

'Good, now I'll come back for you shortly,' he said, as a groaned reply greeted his ears.

'I could get used to living in this receptacle that was once Nathan's body,' he said, chucking the sledgehammer into the crook of his shoulder and walking back over to the casket.

Bringing the sledgehammer slowly down and gripping the handle with both hands, Will began to rock the sledgehammer from side to side in a pendulum motion above the earthen casket, closing his eyelids to the glare of the sun and putting himself into a trance-like state.

A vision slowly came to him, like snapshots with short delays in between each image, of Nathan fleeing from an advance of white blurred apparitions. With each image, an accompany of sharp stabs pierced Will's temples.

Nathan was running flat out, ducking and diving between each tree, puffing and panting.

Still the ghosted blurs of the five angels persisted effortlessly, drifting around the trees, pulling their mangled wings behind them.

Onwards Nathan fled, until at last he came to a clearing where a large, black, Lotus flower shaped object hindered his path, he panicked, and the look of terror spread across his face.

The white phantoms closed in. In a moment of sheer panic, Nate threw himself toward the base of the Lotus, face down into the dirt.

He twisted onto his back and scrambled backwards toward the flower, hiding his head in his hands.

Slowly, the Black Lotus spread open its petals at the base and sharp feathers protruded outwards as it began to spin menacingly around, growing in speed.

Another shooting pain to Will's temples made him double-up in agony. The sledgehammer slipped from his clasp and smashed down into the casket, obliterating it, sending up a poof of ash from inside.

'Arrghh!' Will grimaced in frustration as the vision was cut short.

Picking up the sledgehammer, Will turned on the spot and flung it over the ravine in a rage, where it lodged into the muddy river bank, then he pivoted round and strode over to the van awash with a red mist of anger.

Jamming the button hard to bring the hydraulic lift down, Will yanked down the flap and yanked the wheeled stretcher by the handle, with the occupant strapped tight onboard, clear off the deck.

The folded wheels under the stretcher sprang open and the trolley came to rest at waist height. Will spun the stretcher round and yanked it over to the where the casket lay.

Stooping down, he yanked free the split bag of ash and hoisted it up onto the chest of the occupant upon the stretcher.

Calm began to return to Will, 'Okay, now I'm ready for you,' he said, scooping out a handful of ash and smearing it across the occupant's thrashing face.

'What was your name again?'

Will dragged his palms down across his own face, transferring remnants of ash from his hands, which soaked up the perspiration that clung to his skin. 'That's right, I remember now, Blake! That's your name isn't it?' he said, swiveling the wheeled stretcher around to look into the captured man's eyes.

'Well Blake, I have a story to tell you and one that will seem very farfetched to you, but oh, how every bit of what I'm about to say is true,' Will said, cupping the face of the mortified man before him, whose mouth was messily sutured by string and sewed up tight.

'It all started with my death and will end with yours,' he said, then added 'But slower for you, much slower than mine was I'm afraid, you really were in the right place at the right time,' he chuckled.

Will kicked half the battered casket over the edge of the crag. 'Soon you will be joining the casket Blake, but not until my return, all ravenous and hungry,' he said, scooping up more ash and sprinkling it over the terrified man.

Parts of the battered casket tumbled down the steep slope and clunked in to a semi-submerged, rusted metal object that protruded from the soil by the bed of the river.

The sun glinted off the now disturbed metal item which had on it a faded inscription, but only one line was visible, it read:

TO STAN

THE OASIS OF LIFE

The rest of the inscription though had long since worn away on the flask that had long since been separated from its owner, now just a sharp and twisted forgotten relic, a distant reminder of happier times.

5

EXHUMED

Anastasia stood in the driveway with a mobile phone pressed to her ear and dressed ready for work in a smart business suit, which comprised of a black suit jacket with white stripes running along the edge of her lapels and white pocket flaps. Beneath her jacket she wore a bright orange shirt blouse, adorned with a plain white cravat. Her black trousers were tight fitting and gave her a long leggy look. To finish the look, she fashioned a pair of high gloss, black stilettos.

She watched the police car pull away from her driveway and looked both ways up and down the road to make sure no one was watching. She knew the street was full of busybodies and didn't want to be the subject of gossip, the embarrassment would be too hard to bear, she had a reputation to uphold after all.

Biting her nails, which was a bad habit she had got from her mum Petra, Anastasia waited for her mum to pick up the phone at her end.

After what seemed like five long rings, a quiet voice replied on the other end; 'Hello.'

'Mum it's me, no mum, the other daughter, that's right. Look we have to talk. It's Nate mum, he's stolen my car, yes mum, he's taken the keys and gone out for a joy ride in it. Yes, mum I'm sure, if I had have known that he was going to do something stupid like this, then I never would have agreed to have him stay. Yes mum, I'm well aware he has issues, but this is the final straw. If you see him before I do, then tell him that I have reported him to the authorities... Of course I have mum, what did you expect? You can also tell him not to bother coming back here. If he has so much as scratched or dented my car in any way, then I will personally kill him. No mum I really do mean that, brother or not.'

The phone went silent on Petra's end. 'Mum, you still there? ... Good, sorry, what's that? What do you mean Dustin didn't come home this morning? Well, could it be another callout that he is on? You're sure? Blake's wife told you that? So, they never made it to their callout? What's that?'

Anastasia readjusted the phone to her ear, 'The police have just turned up on your doorstep? Why would they come to you? I explained that Nate was living with me. Okay mum, you have to go, I understand. Look I've contacted work already and explained my situation, so I can swing by yours first...Why? Well they may have information that I need to know about Nate...No, I'm coming over mum, it's decided, I'll tap for an Uber driver and I'll come ASAP,' Anastasia said, hanging up and then speed-dialling work.

Thirty minutes later and Anastasia was dropped off at the bottom of her mum's road.

Rating the hire driver a four star on her mobile app, she clicked confirm and then dialed home. Her husband Arlo immediately picked it up, 'Hi darling, sorry, I overslept, I must have been exhausted. I didn't hear you get up, let alone leave this morning,' he said, apologetically.

'I was going to wake you, but I thought better of it, I did leave you a note on the bedside dresser, did you find it?' Anastasia said, leaning against a wall.

'Yes, yes I did. Don't quite understand it though. You mention something about Nate taking your car and you having to find another way into work. What the hell is that all about? You should have woken me; I could have taken you on my motorcycle and gone out looking for the little prick afterwards.'

'I've reported him to the police babe, so don't worry. I'm just about to go see my mum,' Anastasia said.

'Your mum? You're not due to see her until this evening when we spread the last of your dad's ashes by sending off those fireworks, what are you doing there now? Shouldn't we be looking for your brother?' Arlo said, sounding confused.

'Damn, I had forgotten about tonight. Look there's no time to explain now, just contact me if the police find my car, okay? And get the fireworks packed and ready to go when I get back, can you do that?' Anastasia said, twirling strands of her hair, another trait of her mum's.

'What do you mean get the fireworks ready? I thought you had taken them, because they're not where I left them,' Arlo said, checking a second time.

'Bloody Nathan! He must have taken them. Look, don't go anywhere and keep your eyes and ears open, I'll contact you when I can, love you,' Anastasia said.

'Love you too, just…' Arlo said, but the line went dead, cutting him off.

Anastasia slipped the phone in her pocket in frustration and hurried off up the road, she had barely made it around the corner to her mum's house when a police car passed her way.

With a new found sense of urgency, Anastasia hurried along and dashed up the pathway to the house.

Frantically banging on the door and with no patience for a response, Anastasia fumbled in her pocket for her bunch of keys and quickly located her mum's spare house key, which she jammed into the lock and forced open.

'Mum, mum! Where are you?' she hollered, as she looked in to all the rooms in a panic.

Then she came across Petra in the living room, swigging from a whiskey bottle, with mascara smeared across her eyes and tears rolling down her cheeks.

'You better take a seat, sweetie,' Petra said, motioning to the armchair beside her, not once looking up.

Sitting down and reaching out a hand to grab her mum's leg, Anastasia looked into her mum's eyes, her stomach doing cartwheels; 'What is it mum? What's Nathan done?' she said, gripping her mum's leg.

'Not Nate,' Petra said, in a hollow tone.

'Then what?' Anastasia said, reaching and grabbing her mum's hand.

'The police were called to a disturbance at the cemetery in the early hours of this morning, where your dad is- was, at rest, they found Father Goole, barely alive. They've taken him to intensive care. They're hoping when he recovers, if he recovers, that he can help them with their enquiries,' she blurted.

'In to what mum?' Anastasia said, jiggling a knee nervously.

'They found... They found a body burnt and charred. They say the body was dressed in a funeral operative's attire. Blake's wife had already been to the morgue to identify if it was her husband, she had reported him missing earlier you see, when he never came home after a call from the funeral directors asking where their van was. She said it... wasn't... her hubby. Dusty... Dusty was his on-call partner. They want me to go to the morgue, they think it might be... They think it might be... Dusty,' Petra said, cupping her mouth and sobbing.

Anastasia took the bottle from her mum and reached over, giving her a hug.

'I can't do this again Ana, I can't. I thought I'd settled down again this time,' Petra said, burying her head in her daughter's neck.

As mother and daughter hugged tightly, the pendant containing Stan's ashes that hung around Petra's neck, loosened from its clasp and bounced from her chest where it hit a closed jewelry box that was resting on a nearby coffee table, spilling all its contents over the floor.

Petra leapt in surprise, uncoupling from her daughter's embrace, and slid from the sofa to pick up all her treasured belongings now twinkling from the ray of light that shone on the floor.

Shaking agitatedly, Petra hastily scooped up the items and carefully began to put them back inside the box. 'They're treating it as suspicious circumstances,' Petra said, bringing her head up to look at Anastasia.

'Why is that mum?' Anastasia said, still crying.

'They found your dad's headstone smashed to pieces and a hole in the ground where your father's ashes once were,' she sobbed, smoothing a finger over the glass object that she had just scooped up in her palm.

'You mean?'

'Yes dear, someone has exhumed your dad's ashes,' Petra said, sniffing and deep in shock as she closed her fingers around the pendant tight in her hands.

Anastasia took a deep swig of the bottle, 'Nathan, tell me he's not involved mum?'

'I don't know, I just don't know, but it's a coincidence that if it is Dusty... at the cemetery of your dad then maybe...' Petra trailed off, taking the bottle back and holding the softly vibrating, daisy-infused pendant to her chest.

Anastasia dreaded the worst, especially if her conversation with Arlo regarding the fireworks was anything to go by, *I thought you had taken them, because they're not where I left them!*

She had to keep this from her mum for now, but that would prove tricky, for tonight the fireworks were planned to be let off above the ravine where the accident happened when her dad was but a little boy.

'Did you mention Nate to the police, mum?' Anastasia asked.

'No love, why?'

'No reason, mum, I just think I need to find him to get an explanation of things for me, before the police find him and question him regarding my car, is all,' Anastasia said, with a half-truth to her tone.

And I know just where to go looking for him, she thought to herself.

'You need to call Sally up and get her over to sit with you, so you can have company. You need to tell her what you told me, okay?' Anastasia said, reassuringly.

'But I have to go to the mortuary chapel, love,' Petra said, shaking.

'Not yet, mum. I need to find Nate,' Anastasia said soothingly. 'I will help you with that later,' she added, remorsefully, taking back the bottle.

'Ring Sally.'

'Your sister, of course,' Petra said confused, grabbing her phone from the arm of the sofa.

Unlocking her own phone, Anastasia dialled up Arlo, 'Babe it's me, bring my helmet and jacket and come get me from mum's... I need you to take me somewhere, ...just come, I'll explain everything when you've got here. Ta, bye,'

Both women hung up their phones at the same time, now all Anastasia and Petra could do was wait in a deafening silence.

Petra closed the jewelry box and studied the

remnants of Stan in glass fashioned into a daisy, secretly deliberating whether to put it too into the box, something that Dustin had suggested on many occasions.

An inner struggle told her to resist temptation though.

Petra had always refused to hide it away, as it always been a source of comfort. Although Dustin had refused to let her wear it in his company, so she was forever taking it off and slipping it into her pocket.

Petra gathered that over time the clasp had just worn loose and that was why it had fallen from her neck now, but she couldn't help feeling that a higher power was at work.

Anastasia picked up the sequined jewelry box, flicked it open and found an old trinket with a levered clasp intact inside, 'You could swap over the clasps mum?' she said eyeing the pendant being rolled around in her mum's hand.

Petra reached out her arms and took the box from Anastasia, she then took the pendant and swung it back and forth, debating whether to place it inside the box or not.

'No! Your dad's ashes are in this pendant,' she said softly, twirling it between her fingers, feeling its warmth.

'I never knew you…'

'I want you to have it!' Petra interjected.

'It's brought me great comfort when I've needed it, I hope it brings you comfort whilst you look for your brother,' Petra said, handing it over.

'I can't mum, I…' Anastasia trailed off, as a sense of calm washed over her on touching the glass.

After a fleeting silence, Anastasia said, 'Okay, I promise I will look after dad until I return, then you can have him back.'

Petra helped Anastasia fasten a new clasp to the chain, then the pendant around her neck, and looked at her daughter lovingly, she gave her an approving smile. 'I know you will look after your dad, love,' she said, with tears forming again at the corner of her eyes.

Sitting there in silence, Anastasia played events to come over in her mind of what she would do when she caught up with her brother.

Petra, sharing the silence, prayed that it was not her Dusty that awaited her at the morgue. But if it was, then maybe the vicar in hospital would shed light on what happened last night. The not knowing was tearing her apart from the inside.

Mother and daughter, as if reading one another's thoughts, embraced each other once more and waited.

6

LEUKOCYTES

Ictus pinned Stan tight to the inside of its majestic wings and began to spin on his axis, each individual, razor sharp, steel-like feather on the exterior began to protrude outwards, bathing the interior with sunlight from outside.

Stan got flashing glimpses on each revolution of the outside world, like he was watching a Zoetrope from the inside, in a motion that he had seen when he was a kid. He caught sight of the back of his son cowering before the translucent white fallen angels, that had closed rank around him in a semi-circle, flitting in and out of focus.

Stan went to speak but Ictus cupped a hand to his mouth. 'I recognise all of those angels,' Ictus whispered, and added 'Whilst we maintain motion, they can do us no harm Stan, but for your safety, we must not intervene.'

Stan tried to resist but knew Ictus was far more powerful than he could comprehend.

The dark angel moved its face closer to Stan and through delicate whispers said, 'The tall, slender female of the group is Baso, the squat female to her right is Eosino and the waif to the left is Lymph, she was part of the elite angels that helped secure Petra's Oasis all those years ago.' Stan strained to get a better look but was beginning to get dizzy with each pass.

'The other two females I'm slightly less familiar with, but I think it is Mono, who always paired up with Lymph and Neutro if I'm not mistaken, together they are the five Leukocytes that have been turned by Will to imprison your son and to eradicate you Stan,' Ictus said, waiting for events to play out.

The member of the group known as Eosino stepped forward and squatted down in front of the boy, she regarded the black spinning Lotus for a moment and then turned her attention to Nate.

Nate looked through the gaps in his fingers and let out a fearful wail.

Eosino cocked her head then mimicked Nate's posture, collapsing her mangled wings into her back. She then blended into him, two becoming one.

Like a puppet master commanding a marionette, she now controlled Nate's motions, she brought him to his feet and shuffled him into the throng of her fellow angels.

As the quintet turned and made for the line of trees, the Leukocyte named Baso looked over her shoulder, 'You cannot hide him forever Ictus, we will come for him and when we do, we will feast on his sorrow, or you can save us the trouble and come for the boy, either way, we will devour his very essence,' she challenged, in a hushed but threatening tone. Then they were gone, blending once more into the grove of trees.

Content they were safe from harm for now, Ictus began to slow and released Stan from its icy grip.

'What did she mean by devour my essence?' Stan said, demanding an answer.

Ictus retracted its feathers and came to an abrupt stop. 'It is exactly how they stated it, Stan. They will basically drain your spirit from within, plunging you into the nether.'

'But why are they even here? I never understood white cells and all that, Petra was the neurosurgeon, she would have had the answer. But I'm afraid that I never listened to her much when we were together, especially where work was concerned, I used to just switch off,' Stan said, feeling remorse.

Ictus spread open its wings and pulled Stan in close, rising from the green-tinged pool. 'Because your son has had an onset of schizophrenia due to Will possessing him and suppressing his soul here, the white blood cells that have laid dormant have now come into fruition within his blood stream and are searching to destroy the cause. What they have found is in actual fact a foreign body, i.e. you, as we discussed earlier. You should not exist here. You, they believe are the cause and they the cure.'

'Okay I understand that, but what of poor Nate, what will they do with him?' Stan said, sounding fearful.

'They will do nothing to him, for he is an extension to the host of Will. What they will do, is to stop, at all costs, the threat from spreading any further and reaching Nate. That of course is you.' Ictus said, flapping its wings and carrying them both aloft.

'So, what now Ictus?' Stan said, feeling relieved to be free from the darkness and airborne.

'Now, we leave this island to keep you safe, so we can plan,' Ictus said, soaring higher.

'Then we assemble an army and return?' Stan asked, expectedly.

'Yes, and I know just where to start,' Ictus said, as it beat its wings to the wind.

Stan became a wreck of mixed emotions, elation and fear, for he knew what Ictus meant.

It had been such a long time ago since he had returned there. The last time he had lost the fight to Will and ended up back on Earth, for only a small matter of time, before finally his life on Earth was taken.

He had been everywhere and anywhere since, but he was always forbidden from going there, patience had never been his virtue but that was what had transpired. Now it seemed that his longing would finally be fulfilled.

They were going back to his wife's island of her subconscious mind, where he knew his father-in-law was the soul guardian, along with his beloved leopard, Heparin.

He couldn't wait to see how much they had all changed.

7

WILDFIRE

It had all started out quite mundane and just like any other ordinary day in the afterlife, for the once fallen angel Nathaniel.

But now, as he looked back from the madness of his fellow angels flying backwards and forwards against the black smoky sky to the raging fires burning against the backdrop of the blizzard tempest, all he could do was reminisce and wonder how he got to this point.

He thought back to the middle of his day, having just gotten supplies.

The fully restored angel and sole guardian and gatekeeper over his daughter's Island Oasis, Nathaniel trudged drearily through the deep snow drifts that rose waist-height across the open plains.

His companion, a large and muscular leopard, trailed close behind him, shaking snow from his paws as they both battled the blizzard blowing East across their path with the whistling wind deafening their approach.

A net bag of half-frozen seagulls swung around

the waist of the fearsome-looking Nathaniel and the shivering leopard licked its lips from behind, watching the tantalising treats jostle around.

The leopard nudged the net, pushing it into its master's side.

Nathaniel, whose giant wings were folded up over his head to give himself shelter from the harsh conditions, parted a wing and dropped it to his side to look over his shoulder, taking the full force of the blizzard to his snow-covered, left bearded cheek and smiled.

He yanked the net round to his front and through freezing fingers pulled it apart to retrieve a bird from within.

Nathaniel tossed it toward the leopard, 'There you go Nimodi, enjoy,' he said, turning his face away again from the ice cold wind and bringing his wing back over his head.

Heparin, or Nimodi as Nathaniel called him, catching the bird in his mouth, crunched through the seagull's rib cage, releasing the darkened blood to seep down his throat. He then tossed the bird up into the air in a playful manner to catch it again, sending blood spattering in every direction across the brilliant white powder, but he flung it too wide, the bird fell away into the deep drift.

The leopard stopped in his tracks and swiped a paw into the freezing snow to reach the bird that sunk from view further down into the snow. The distance between him and his master was growing now, and the snow had all but claimed the bird from view.

Nimodi gave a saddened final look and bounded

off to catch the angel up. On doing so, he found his master standing at the edge of a wide chasm with a snow-laden, rickety, wooden, slatted bridge spanning its gorge.

'Almost home, Nimodi,' Nathaniel shouted over the screeching winds. 'We will have to be careful with this crossing though, it looks a little treacherous to me. Shame I can't just fly over but that's impossible in these conditions,' he said, turning to the leopard and rubbing the big cat's chin.

'Still, it was worth the trek to get this haul, these should keep me revitalized for ages,' he added, lifting up the bag of birds and stepping out onto the wildly swinging bridge.

Tentatively, Nathaniel and Nimodi inched their way over the chasm, careful not to slip through the gaps in between the wooden planks or out through the sides of the rope railings.

Having crossed half-way, Nathaniel stopped, wiped snow from his brows and looked out to the dark grey outline of an island on the horizon.

The island he knew to be that of his grandson Nate, that had separated from his mother's island many years ago by a delicate bond that was once a long narrow pathway of sand. But that had long since been claimed by the sea when mother and son had drifted apart to make way for a new island that drifted across their path and had taken root on the boy's mother's shoreline, in turn pushing the boy's island further out to sea. That island belonged to his new son-in-law, Dustin.

Nathaniel sighed heavily and prayed that his son-in-law Stan would uphold his promise and make everything right once more. But this new island that had joined his daughter's seemed to have a stronger bond than his daughter and previous son-in-law ever had and that worried Nathaniel more than anything, for he knew that Stan had no knowledge of this new island existing, as he had not visited here for many years. So much had changed in a short time and not all for the better, at least that was what Nathaniel believed.

Having loitered on the bridge for a little longer, Nathaniel decided to move on but only with the insistence of Nimodi, who was slipping and sliding behind him and decided in frustration to gnaw on Nathaniel's leg, not just for grip or safety but also to get a move on as Nimodi was feeling a touch of vertigo.

Pushing on, soon they were across to the other side where snow-capped trees in a cluster greeted them at a forked path. Nathaniel knew to the left was the Oasis hidden behind the trees, tucked away in a secret meadow guarded by fifty strong angels. To the right was a path that led to an overlooking cliff to the sea below, which passed by steps that cut into the side of the cliff leading down to the shoreline where the new island had joined his daughter's one.

Nathaniel had watched warily for many years the advance of this new island, inching closer every day until it had beached on his daughter's island, creating a larger land mass.

Nathaniel knew that his daughter had moved on with her life and taken on a new life partner. But as of yet, he did not know what ramifications it would have for Stan and his mission once he had found out that the love of his life had taken another.

The once fallen angel had been curious as to whom the island belonged to and longed to take a sneak peek upon it. But he had vowed to never leave his daughter's island for fear of William Last's untimely return.

What Nathaniel did find odd whilst he observed the merger over the years, was just how colder his daughter's island had become. The temperature had dropped rapidly in the last few years just as this new island that beached her island had warmed in temperature to become a tropical climate.

As for his grandson's island, it was sad watching it become barren and lifeless. But that had been expected due to a takeover by a despot like Will. But that seemed so long ago as it had drifted almost out of sight.

Nathaniel spread open his wings and beat them hard against the prevailing winds, showering Nimodi in the dusty snow.

The big cat didn't seem amused, and slinked off down the steps in disgust.

Nathaniel chuckled to himself and folded them to his back making his way off in the other direction toward the Oasis.

From out of the blue, an almighty crack sent a shockwave through the trees, bending them over and relinquishing them of snow, in turn catching them alight, throwing Nathaniel off his feet into a large mound of snow that hissed against the heatwave that followed.

He thought it came from the other island, but he couldn't be sure. His first instinct was to chase after Nimodi and go take a look but better judgement took hold, as it could be quite possible that his daughter's Oasis could be under siege or the other island was a ruse to get him to go there to leave his daughter's one exposed and vulnerable.

Making his mind up, Nathaniel raced through the burning trees and headed for the Oasis, hoping that Nimodi would find his way back safely.

Just as he neared the Oasis opening, a mass flapping of thunderous wings joined the commotion as all the residing angels took flight in unison towards the now darkened skies.

So here Nathaniel was now, frozen in time and undecided on his next cause of action.

Making a snap decision, he beat his wings and took to the sky, homing in on the nearest angel he could find, the smoke filled his lungs as he struggled to get his words out, 'Is it safe? Is my daughter's Oasis in danger?' he rasped, knowing that the scar over his trachea had never fully healed from an encounter long ago and was now aggravated by the smoke inhalation.

'Yes, we are secure here. We've ascertained that the blast has come from the exterior of our defenses, from the connected island. Look over there, it has split in half and is now a burning inferno,' the angel said, pointing behind him.

Nathaniel had been here before. It all seemed quite familiar.

'We need to put out our fires and stop that island's fires from reaching this island,' Nathaniel said, through hoarse words.

'We are already on it, but we could use your help too as this wildfire is spiraling out of control,' the angel said, turning to regroup with the others.

Nathaniel was torn, he knew he had to secure his daughter's Oasis, but he could also see Nimodi below making his way over to the neighbouring island. But above all, if whoever inhabited that island was truly his daughter's new life partner, then he owed it to her to save them whatever the cost, even if it went against Stan's wishes, for he knew in his heart that it was the right thing to do.

Deciding to help his brothers and sisters and, against his better judgement, Nathaniel put the consequences of not helping the victim below far from his mind and took off at speed.

Nathaniel was more afraid for Nimodi than anything else although he was sure the big cat could look after himself. Maybe he would have time for a rescue mission later or maybe Nimodi would get lucky in the meantime.

Either way this powder keg of events couldn't have come at a worse time.

8

HEARSEMAN OF THE APOCALYPSE

With his keen sense of hearing, the nimble but cautious leopard leapt over fallen burning trees that sank down into the turbulent sea, sizzling and spitting on contact, extinguishing the bright embers infused within the bark as they slowly turned the sea a cloudy charcoal grey.

Dodging fire balls that screamed in arcs over the ashen haze, the big cat whipped his tail away from harm as he sprinted through and around the devastation of the island.

Engulfed in the hot searing flames, the island's splintered mass was slowly being devoured by the icy cold, raging torrent from below, choking out its existence.

The leopard noticed an outline of a lone figure in the distance who seemed to be struggling to hold onto a felled tree that was rocking violently against the battering waves in the middle of a freshly created basin.

The soot-covered leopard stopped and scoured the sky to see if the bird man had followed him to apologize with treats for covering him in the white cold stuff earlier. But he was nowhere to be found.

Smelling the fear and dread all around, Heparin hesitated before he would react as his fur bristled with trepidation.

The leopard missed his original companion, as he had not seen him for some time. But somehow his more recent and longer standing companion was trying very hard to win him over with a plentiful supply of nutritious birds. He just wondered why the bird man called him Nimodi and not the name he preferred, that of Heparin.

Sniffing the air and sensing even greater danger ahead, the lean and very sleek Leopard approached the noisy human with apprehension, knowing that he hadn't been spotted by him yet.

Heparin's thoughts were that if he saved this human then a great deed would be done, and such deeds would get him more recompense.

Pacing backwards and forwards, the leopard eyed the white froth of the sea lapping against the slope of the crumbling and scorched earth he was standing on.

A large chasm spread out before him about a mile across the basin. The far side of the burning island had risen into the sky, pushing the split at its centre further down into the rushing sea that bubbled ferociously, causing the figure on the bobbing floating tree to keep losing his grip.

Heparin looked back the way he had traveled and noticed how his half of the island also had begun to rise at its outer rim, pulling it up and away from Petra's island beyond.

Like a tide coming in, Heparin began to back off from the encroaching sea that lapped at his paws.

Without warning, a large chunk of the land gave way underfoot and plunged Heparin into the salty drink.

Thrashing blindly, Heparin made for the figure at the centre of the turmoil, trying to keep his head above the waves that threatened to spill into his maw. Using his sharp claws, he dug them into the tree's bark to pull himself up and onto the tree's exposed dry side.

The figure, a mildly charred and burnt man, shrieked in terror and let go of the tree, where he began to wave his arms around in a panic and tried to swim to a neighbouring piece of drift wood, gulping and choking on the frenzied sea.

Fighting hard to stay upright, Heparin spread his entire frame across the tree and watched as the man knocked all manner of floating objects out of his way as he panicked to locate a hand-hold on a nearby charred floating tree.

It was then that Heparin got some faint recognition of the disfigured man before him. He wasn't overly certain, but the man looked very similar to the one that used to feed him every now and again when he was but a kitten. A tyrant of a man that had made him very ill with excruciating pain, that had slowly over a short time made him succumb to this other life in this alien world by way of poison.

Heparin gave a roar of anger at the man and for his own foolishness for wanting to help someone who had done him harm. Tired, wet and miserable,

THE OASIS OF LIFE

Heparin now found himself in this precarious situation through a bad decision.

Looking around the basin and to nearby floating debris, Heparin tried to look for a path so he could leap from tree to tree to get back to dry land and be free of this nightmare. But something new caught his eye; something large, sinewy and grey buffeted the tree Heparin was on from just below the shallows, causing the tree he was on to spin in a wide arc. Then it snared another floating tree nearby before it then disappeared beneath the surface, briefly taking the tree with it, only to resurface again closer to the man who had ended Heparin's once happy life on Earth with the tree popping from the surface and drifting away.

The fledgling burnt man in the water also noticed the advancing grey mass approaching and began screaming in a high audible pitch that pierced Heparin's sensitive ears.

Heparin watched in awe and fascination at the pitiful man who suddenly became quiet and still as he treaded water, looking around uneasily. Then in a flash the man was gone, pulled down beneath the ebb and flow of the waves just as the two halves of the island began to slide further into the depths after him.

Fearing he would be next, or worse, crushed by the two opposing plates of the oncoming island crashing into one another, Heparin seized an opportunity and leapt onto closing coarse woody debris, bounding off of each as he snaked his way to and fro, feeling the searing heat of the lit island plates converging on his ever-changing position.

The path ahead though began to close, cutting off his escape route as the two plates collided, sending an updraft of air to push the blistering fires skyward.

Trees that were once vertical, embedded in the island on both sides, were now horizontal and started to plummet with the motion of the sinking adjacent plates.

Abandoning the driftwood that he had held onto with dear life, Heparin leapt onto one such tree whist avoiding the rising flames and climbed from tree to tree, moving upwards between the plates, trying to move quicker than the rapid descent would allow.

As both fiery plates hit the sea below, snuffing out the heat, steam quickly took their place and rose upwards causing visibility to be nigh on impossible for Heparin's ascent. Fire above and steam rising from below filled him with lack of hope for survival, the air became dense and every breath became nauseating with smoke.

But just as all seemed lost, the two halves of the falling island abruptly stopped dead, ending with a large cracking sound.

Heparin slowed his pace and waited for the air above to clear so he could see how longer his journey would take, but something seemed off as a creeping feeling washed over him.

Looking down from the perch he was on, the steam dispersed a little and what then greeted him was not something he was expecting. There below him and clinging onto a rooted tree for dear life, was the charred man whom he thought had been lost to a watery grave.

Heparin went to move off with no regard for the vile human when he sensed the man was looking across to the opposite plate with a fear in his eyes that Heparin had never seen before.

At first it was hard to make out through the billowing smoke what the man was looking at, but then slowly and surely, Heparin quickly realised the predicament they had now found themselves in. There across from them, contorted in a behemoth form of twisted limbs and conjoined rotten grey bodies with a hundred sunken eyes staring back, was the most grotesque monster that Heparin had ever seen.

Heparin identified a familiar face from the centre of the hideous grey bulbous mass that was now moving in unison up through the hanging trees and it made him want to bolt for freedom.

Smiling back at him through viscid, rotten grey lips was a disfigured female face that Heparin had briefly encountered a long time ago. There was no mistaking who it was; Venous had returned and with her a vengeful army of grey matter that were hell bent on claiming Heparin and the man for their own ranks.

A bulking great monster, created from a mass hemorrhage when Dustin had been inflicted by a firework on Earth that had split open his cranium at force, now manifested here as a nightmare, bringing lost souls together from the sea.

'I see you've found a friend then, Dustin!' Venous gurgled, through salty wet lips, shifting the weight of the large grey mass.

'All of this is brought about by you Dusty, my hearse man of the apocalypse,' she mocked, 'Oh well, time to swell our numbers now then I guess,' she added, before throwing the bulk of her mass towards them.

Dustin slipped and fell with shock into the dark cavernous sea below. Heparin watched him splash into the depths, turned and poised himself ready for attack, retracting and protracting his claws.

Heparin didn't understand what this pulsating, bulbous mass had just said, but he was sure it didn't sound good.

9

ISLAND RETREAT

Keeping one wary eye on the horizon, Nathaniel beat his great wings to fan back the fires that torched the snow-covered canopies. With his band of angel companions spread out in a wide arc doing the same, the blaze was slowly being contained, helped also in part by the blizzard that had since changed direction and was now blowing back out to sea.

Witnessing the island inferno in the distance spread far and wide with both parts of the severed island now converging towards one another lifting high into the sky, Nathaniel prayed for the leopard's safety.

Sensing Nathaniel's anguish, a female angel swooped over to him and grabbed his shoulders, 'We can manage here, you should go and find your big cat,' she yelled through the storm, in an accent that Nathaniel always admired.

Nathaniel looked into her big brown eyes and wiped the powdered snow from her dark skin, 'Thank you Iyanla, so long as you're sure you can cope here?' he said through chattering teeth.

'Ha, without you? Of course we can. Now go,' she said, stroking his cheek, before releasing her grasp and letting the harsh wind blow her away to regroup with the others.

Smiling inwardly, Nathaniel beat his wings and dispersed a few feathers, taking flight to the doomed island in the distance that was now showing its underside of earth with gushing water showering down to the sea below.

*

Dragging her bloated, slippery and abhorrent rotten form along the cluster of trees that sagged under the hulking great mass, Venous commanded her spliced counterparts to work simultaneously to move together as one unit but with disastrous consequences.

As the shambling collective of lost souls pulled and pushed in different directions, the almost comical but frightening animated limbs of certain individuals came away, snagging on branches with a sickening squelch. Loose slimy arms and legs rained down onto a horrified Dustin who was thrashing in the cold sea below.

Venous, frustrated and livid, yelled out to her cohort of evil subservients, 'When I tell you to do something, you damn well do it!' she demanded, with wails and moans of assimilation as her response.

Hissing and spitting from his attack stance nearby, Heparin decided to strike first. Dashing forward and leaping from the tree to his target with outstretched claws, his talons pierced the bulbous squishy flesh of an exposed torso belonging to a withered and emaciated woman, who shrieked like a banshee as her blackened organs spilled out through the sliced open cavity of her chest.

Heparin, in one smooth fluid motion, ripped open her throat with his jaw, turned and pushed off the mass with his muscular hind legs back to the opposite tree, where he then turned to face his prey with his tail swishing blindly behind him.

Against a growl of defiance from the agile cat, Venous knew better than to take on this challenger as she knew the cat was more comfortable with trees than she and so would have the advantage.

'Down!' she yelled 'Down to the human below, we claim his soul for our own, leave the beast alone.'

Dustin, who could not tear his eyes away from the spectacle above, suddenly found a new vigour of strength and made for a crack of light between the two islands, with a hope of escaping this unholy hell that he had awoken in.

Mustering all her strength and will from her kin, the mutated form of Venous threw her entire weight away from the grove and plummeted down with an almighty splash into the sea, a short distance from Dustin who yelled in surprise.

In an instant, the assemblage of relentless grey, ravenous dead cells was upon him, grabbing hold of his arms and legs to pull him into their embrace below the water line.

Leeching onto Dustin's struggling body like a parasite burrowing into a host, the grey mass of Venous began to absorb his very soul.

*

Far overhead, Nathaniel circled the two halves of the island protruding from the sea like hands clasped in prayer, looking for an opening that was not barred by flames or thick dense smoke.

Spotting an opening, he dropped his wings to his side and nose-dived though the fissure. The deeper his descent the darker the hazard became as thick black smoke and tangled branches obscured his vision causing him to twist and turn to avoid being impaled on ripped trees jutting out from both sides.

A misjudged turn knocked Nathaniel off course and caused him to spiral into a nearby tree covered in a blazing inferno. The once brilliant white of his delicate feathered wings were now grey and heavy with soot ignited from the leaping flames, forcing him to turn onto his back for fear of the flames scorching his face as he spread them out wide to his side.

Sailing past the leopard in a fireball and continuing his out-of-control plummet, Nathaniel caught sight of the cat's deep, icy blue eyes staring back at him in wonder and awe from the darkness.

Arms outstretched and wings leaving behind a smoke trail from their tips, Nathaniel closed his eyes tight as he braced himself for impact.

Heparin, whose curiosity had gotten the better of him, had begun working his way back down, leaping from tree to tree with a heavy thud following the trail of the falling angel. He suddenly stopped on hearing a sloppy squelch and mortified screams rise up from far below.

His master Nathaniel had collided with the

gruesome and horrific mass of Venous and her maddening throng, sending them all reeling to the depths of the sea which in turn severed the contact between Venous' mass and Dustin's weak and fragile defeated state.

Then all became silent from below the wispy plume of the smoke rising above his head, giving Heparin a chance to abandon the island via the dead calm of the sea.

By the time Heparin had gingerly made it off the doomed island to the safety of Petra's beach, the murky sea had become eerily still with no sign of anyone anywhere.

10

PENNANCE

Grief-stricken and going out of her mind with worry for Anastasia and Nate, Petra felt that she could not just sit around and do nothing. So, deciding to motivate herself, which took a massive amount of time and effort, she had decided to take a trip to the hospital where she now sat in her car with the engine running.

Plucking up the courage, she pulled .out her mobile phone and made a call to the coroner's office, given to her by the police on their earlier visit, and waited intently for someone to answer. Her hand shook uncontrollably with her phone in hand and her heart pounding heavily in her chest.

Arranging to see Dusty, if it was him, was the last thing on her mind to do, but somehow having gone through the same heartache with Stan had made her desensitized to every presumptuous outcome she could imagine, praying that deep down that it wasn't truly him waiting for her at the morgue.

In her absent-mindedness though, she had forgotten she had invited her daughter Sally over to her house and now found herself sitting in the hospital grounds carpark alone, lonely and confused, having an empty, soulless conversation with an unhappy porter of her insistence to see her late husband at short notice. Her day had been spent coasting on autopilot just to get here.

With further directions of where the mortuary was by the porter, Petra had put the car in gear and, after some mindless driving, found herself pulling up to a pedestrian crossing to allow an elderly couple to cross. She looked around to the blue signposted markings, biting her nails.

The mortuary pointed to the left up ahead and a collection of other department signs pointed to the right. One of the signs on the right stood out more than the others and that was signposted 'Intensive Care Unit'.

The realisation of seeing Dusty, if it really was him, slowly dawned and scared the hell out of her. Feelings of guilt and emptiness took hold as she recounted losing Stan, having lived through this nightmare once before.

Deciding to put off the morgue for now, Petra turned hard right and went to find herself a parking space. Reasoning that she could pull some strings to go and see the minister who was in intensive care, hoping that he was making a recovery and not in bad shape.

She rationed that he could put her mind at ease for what he had seen at the cemetery concerning both Dusty and Nate, if Nate was indeed there, and maybe just maybe, her atonement for remarrying would be granted by the priest, as she had harboured the guilt for all these years and now felt that she was being punished for her past actions and wanted absolution.

She prayed that Father Goole was in a fit state to help her by easing her conscious.

Petra parked up and turned off the engine, not even thinking about buying a ticket. Doctors and nurses were encouraged to park and ride into their place of work, but it was never that simple when long hours interfered with their days. Massive parking fines were not unheard of and Petra figured one more would not make an awful difference.

She went to exit the car when her phone suddenly rang. Petra stared at the caller ID for some time before she answered, 'Sally, hello darling. What can I do for you?' she said, with her fingers still shaking, clasped round the phone.

Sally started talking but her words were lost on Petra.

'I'm at the hospital dear, I'm going to see the Father Goole,' she said, cutting her daughter off.

The voice on the other end echoed from the phone as Petra dropped it from her ear, lost in thought. 'Mum, I'm worried about you, I came to see you as asked but you weren't there when I arrived. I feared the worst. What's going on, mum? Look, I'm coming over to you now, just stay where you are, okay? Mum are you there?'

Petra, with her mind elsewhere, had already hit the power off button on her phone, thrown it into the door-well and exited the car, before briskly navigating through the parked cars, with the burden weighing heavy on her mind.

It didn't take long to locate the whereabouts of Father Goole as Petra was well recognised in her field and had sway with a majority of the staff at the hospital, even though she was warned of the minister's unstable condition.

Moments later, she found herself outside his room and knocked gently on the door, peering through the glass window that was housed in its centre.

The chubby man in the hospital bed was, to her short-fleeting joy, alive, but looked a little pale and clammy, rigged up to the machines keeping him stable. Petra knew she shouldn't go in as he needed rest and care, but her overwhelming urge to get answers swayed her better judgement. She pushed open the door and swept in unseen.

The minister showed no hint of awareness as Petra took a hold of his hand and sat down on the bed at his side.

'Father, it's Petra, you know my husband Dustin. He works with you occasionally,' Petra spoke softly.

The Reverend's pulse quickened and his closed eyes twitched leaving Petra with the sad realisation that he was in a coma. Further memories of Stan in his vegetative state all those years ago made her burst into a flood of tears.

Petra lay her head on his gently beating chest and was greeted with a frail wheezing sound from within. She found herself between a rock and a hard place, on one hand her second husband could potentially be in the adjacent building, leaving her to face the cold harsh reality of her predicament that he would no longer be in her life, or to be reminded of her first husband's suffering when he was once in a coma and his fate was uncertain.

Petra sat up and began to talk, hoping that the Reverend could still hear her, 'I'm sorry Father, I came to ask if you would be able to tell me about, you know, what happened at the cemetery? But I realise now that I have made a mistake coming here, I'm putting off the inevitable,' Petra said, glancing around nervously.

Reverend Goole's fingers twitched as if he was trying to respond, giving Petra a glimmer of hope.

'It's just that my son is missing, and my husband is feared…' Petra trailed off.

'The police said I need to identify my second husband, for they believe he is… dead,' she added defeated.

Reverend Goole, fighting with his inner demons to awaken, let out a deep sigh that Petra took for a sign.

Petra burst into tears again and sobbed.

'I really wish someone could tell me what happened, Father. I need to know if my missing son had anything to do with what happened at the cemetery,' she pleaded through muffled tones.

As if a miracle had happened, Father Goole opened his eyes, found her face and brushed her cheek with a frail hand.

To Petra's jubilation, he proceeded to cup her chin, pulling her gaze up to his, 'My faith has been greatly tested, what I saw will haunt me forever,' he said wheezing. 'I saw a youth with the eyes of the devil control the weather, I then saw him command a league of angels to carry out his evil work and I witnessed a great sacrifice from a wholly spirit... If the youth is your son and your husband the father of the boy, then there is no penance for him so fitting for such a heinous act,' he added sporadically.

Petra looked at him disbelievingly and in shock.

'I pray that this is not the case,' he added further, struggling for breath and trying to locate the button to call for assistance.

Petra, sitting up, now wiped her eyes and looked at the Reverend perplexed, 'Dustin is not the biological father of Nate, my son. Stan passed away a long time ago. I remarried and have lived with the guilt ever since,' she said, eyes misting over.

Reverend Goole's breathing became shallower as he grabbed hold tight of Petra's shoulders, doubling up in pain.

He then pushed her away abruptly and reached for something at the side of his bed.

Petra, slow to act, couldn't fathom what was happening with the Reverend as he suddenly gave out a yell and collapsed back onto the bed, stiff as a board.

It was then it dawned on her, seeing his hand grasping the call button in his hand. The Reverend had had another stroke and was now unconscious again beside her.

Petra, in alarm and believing she was to blame, fled from the room having a full-blown panic attack, just as two nurses came hurrying up the corridor behind her.

11

QUIETUS

Tearing up the tarmac on a Triumph Bonneville T120, rode Arlo with Anastasia as his pillion passenger.

Having already discussed the destination to her husband, Anastasia held on tight around his waist and scanned the river bank running adjacent to their left, looking for the turning that would take them off the highway.

The opening would lead them to a small bridge that cut across the river, to take them over and on to an overgrown road byway that had all but been forgotten by time.

The winding dusty road that lay ahead was now only used by horse riders and teenagers looking for thrills on their dirt bikes.

Mother Nature had finally claimed back the earth from the advancement of the ever-increasing modern roadway, Motormobile, in turn creating a forgotten tribute to the many lives that the river had claimed in the past.

There was a time when the byway was a major

road until a minibus carrying school children had avoided a head-on collision with a vehicle coming the opposite way and sent them all, bar one, to their unfortunate deaths over the ravine to the icy river below.

The road was deemed unsafe and too costly to rectify and ended up being closed to make way for a safer alternative highway to be crafted on the opposite side of the river.

Anastasia's dad had been the only survivor of the unfortunate accident when he was but a boy and she knew only too well that the very same river had finally claimed his life in adulthood many years later.

It was only fitting that the spot the minibus had gone over, which was a short distance from where her dad had died, would be the place to scatter his ashes by fireworks on this very night. She couldn't help but feel a strange coincidence of re-occurring events that would lead her there now to find her brother. It all seemed connected somehow.

Tapping Arlo on the shoulder and pointing to the short steel bridge that crossed the Mala Sort river up ahead, the pair peeled off to make their way over to the rusted bridge and onwards to the treacherous inclined and abandoned road, gunning the engine as the motorcycle kicked up loose chippings.

Eventually the pair came to a clearing and caught sight of a black removal van parked under a large oak tree high above the ravine that acted like a sentry overlooking the river far below. Arlo pulled up to the van's rear and turned off the engine.

By the time he had removed the key and pulled

the motorcycle onto its stand, Anastasia had already dismounted, removed her helmet and was walking up to the van for closer inspection.

Arlo took a bike chain from around his neck, locked it through the rear wheel, before hastily running up alongside Ana, pulling her back by the shoulder, he put a finger to his lips inside the open faced helmet and gestured her to stay put whilst he crept around to the cab of the van.

Anastasia went to protest that the motorbike would have alerted anyone close by to their oncoming arrival when suddenly her husband had returned shrugging his shoulders, motioning to her that it was empty.

Removing his helmet now, Arlo noticed a splintered box on the edge of the ravine and went over to take a look, leaving Anastasia to inspect the van further.

On the side of the van, set out in bold Times New Roman italics, was lettering that read QUIETUS INDEPENDENT FUNERAL GROUP with a symbol of a musical quarter rest note underneath.

Running her hand across the embossed lettering, Anastasia became aware of the silence that hung in the air all around as a light wind buffeted the van, causing a low-emitting hum.

Letting her fingers slip from the wording, Anastasia walked round to the rear of the van and peered into the top half of the hold where she found it to be empty with a strange pungent odour that wafted out to greet her. She wrinkled her nose and leant back, a chill traveled down her spine as a fleeting thought appeared in her mind's eye of how many deceased people must have been transported within the confines of the van over the years and if it could be haunted. Slightly crouching now, she peered into the bottom half of the hold and heard a tapping sound from in the far corner.

A large gasp from Arlo made her jump in fright, she turned her attention to him and gave him a scolding look just as a crow flew out from the van and skimmed her head, before settling on a nearby tree.

Anastasia let out a scream in fright and raced over to Arlo's side where he was crouched down and holding something in his hands, obscured from her vision.

With a saddened look, Arlo held up the remnants of the shattered box with a dented gold plaque nailed to the surface, on it was engraved a name. Anastasia, still flustered, didn't need to look twice, as the name STANLEY PALMER was more than clear enough to read.

The crow watched with its beady eyes from afar and gave a cawing sound which signalled another crow to join it on an overhanging branch. Fascinated, the pair of crows looked on as they sensed a strange vibration in the air emitting from the pendant around Anastasia's neck. They looked at each other oddly and hopped further out along the branch to get a closer look.

Finally, dropping the casket and standing up, Arlo pulled his wife into his arms and gave her a warm embrace, with her tears splashing onto his leather lapel.

Frozen to the core and with a rage like no other Arlo had ever experienced from his wife, Anastasia released her grasp and clenched her fists, her perfectly painted and manicured nails slicing her palms and drawing blood.

Before Arlo could say anything of comfort, Anastasia suddenly became agitated and pushed past him to the edge of the ravine where she then screamed at the top of her lungs.

But then, all of a sudden, she immediately froze and squinted to look at something far below that Arlo could not yet see. Then in an instant she hopped off the edge and began to descend down the steep slope to the river.

Arlo looked to his wife in bewilderment and then caught her gaze, she was transfixed on a large apparatus nestled down by the river's embankment, semi-submerged in the water.

He watched her clumsily make her way down the hard slope, past the splinters of the rest of the destroyed casket and watched her try to compose her stance as one of her high heels sank into the dirt where it broke free from the shoe.

Racing after her, he found himself sliding onto his backside in haste, thankful that his leather jacket gave him some protection from the embedded stone that jutted from the slope to tear at his back.

By the time Arlo caught up with Anastasia she was already yanking the trolley from the river and onto dry land with a determination that he had never seen her do before.

Her stilettos were caked in mud; her trousers were

ripped along with her coat and her makeup had run across her cheeks. Arlo, fearing for her sanity, jumped into the freezing cold water and helped her pull the stretcher free from its resting place and caught his wife shivering, but he wasn't sure if it was from the freezing river or her emotional state.

Spinning the trolley around to face them, husband and wife looked at each other puzzled and then back to the red plastic matting of the cover on the gurney.

Dark red blood spatter glistened on its surface and both partners feared the worst, both secretly praying that it was blood from an already dead corpse and not from the living or recently dead, judging by the amount of the thick liquid on show.

Arlo looked at the severed straps swinging idly from two of the three positions on either side of the stretcher. The belt clip was in tact at the foot end but not clasped shut, whereas the middle strapping and shoulder bonding were clearly cut away. Someone was clearly restrained upon the gurney and had most definitely cut themselves loose but at what cost, the blood was surely a sign of a struggle and it put both Arlo and Anastasia at unease.

It was then that Anastasia spotted a tarnished and rusted metal flask that had been stamped into the wet mud by a footprint tread at the side of the river, from where they had just pulled the trolley out.

Arlo caught her eye and intercepted it, pulling it free with a squelch. He turned it over in his palm and dropped it in fright into the fast-flowing water.

Another coincidence! He thought, as a blood-soaked and engraved flask that was turned face up in view sank into the watery depths and was then washed away. There was no mistaking what it had read: TO STAN.

Anastasia couldn't quite make out the inscription as it passed from view, 'What did it say on it?' she asked.

Arlo covered his mouth in horror, then said 'I think you're right; Nate was here, and I think that your dad is trying to tell us something from beyond the grave or something,' he said with a nervous laugh.

Anastasia slumped against the trolley, 'What? What are you talking about? Don't make horrid jokes, I don't understand…'

Arlo took her arm in his and turned her around, 'Look,' he said pointing, 'footprints in the mud trailing away down the river, they look fresh, we should follow them,' he added, trying to deflect the conversation away.

Anastasia gave him a scolding look, 'If my brother was here, then what the bloody hell has he got himself into this time?' she said, then added 'If you're holding something back Arlo, then I ought to damn well know what it is,' she said, pointing a finger at him.

Arlo let his arms drop to his sides and was about to speak when he then caught sight of another object further along the river bank, 'It can't be, can it?' he said to himself.

Anastasia creased her face at him 'No, don't you change the subject,' she said, looking first at him then to what he was looking at.

'The tracks lead past that object over there, look,' he said, pointing away.

'Those footprints look deep,' Anastasia said, puzzled at her husband's strange behaviour, noticing her footprints had not made those kind of deep impressions in the mud. 'But what is that sticking out of the mud?' she said, squinting to the falling sun to get a better look.

'I think I know. Come on Ana, we better hurry,' Arlo said. 'Just mind how you go,' he added.

'What did you see on that metal shard?' she asked, perplexed and refusing to budge until she got an answer.

'Later Ana, I will tell you later,' Arlo said, as he pulled her along to make their way on the trail of the footprints.

Reluctantly Ana agreed, 'Later,' she said, with determination and stubbornness.

Back up on the ridge from where they came, the black removal van swayed against the intensifying wind which increased in momentum, creating a crescendo of a shrill humming noise.

The two crows that had remained silent up until now cawed to one another and then descended down to the ravine's edge to a pile of ash that was scattered in the brush. The crows hopped into the ash and flapped their wings, covering themselves in the remains and sending plumes of it up into the air, then they scooped large quantities of it up into their beaks.

Traces of the cremated ash that had laid dormant up until now in the undergrowth, and of which had gone unnoticed by the couple, wafted up into the wind and was carried aloft into the opening at the rear of the van, where upon arrival, an updraft of wind that drifted over the lip of the ravine and blown the door shut, trapping the ash within its makeshift tomb.

The wind then died down and the humming ceased as if the melodious tune had reached its coda.

The crows, fresh from tasting the ash that saturated their tongues, beat their wings and took off after the couple, leaving the Quietus removal van deathly silent.

One of the crows, as if it had gathered up information, parted ways with the first and flew off ahead, passing above Arlo who had pulled an object from the mud.

'He's definitely around here somewhere, Ana. Look at this, it's my sledgehammer and no mistake,' he said, brandishing it aloft, 'I bet you this is what he used to smash your dad's casket,' he said, realising too late what he had just said.

'I'm going to bloody kill him when I see him,' Anastasia said, storming off ahead with steely determination.

Arlo watched her leave, paused, then rested the sledgehammer on his shoulder before hurrying after her.

12

CELESTIAL BURIAL

Some time earlier, carrying the ravaged body of Blake over his shoulder, William Last, in possession of Nate's body, controlled each movement of the teenage boy with deft vigour.

He heard the sound of the motorbike in the distance carrying across the river and recognised the unmistakable roar of Nate's brother-in-law's Triumph. He knew that Nate's sister wouldn't be far behind. He cursed, for he knew he had wasted too much time already.

Stopping in his tracks he called out to his fallen angels, Mono and Neutro, who upon request appeared in the sky above in the guise of crows.

Will hadn't been comfortable summoning them into being as it had only left Eosino, Baso and Lymph guarding Nate. But it had been impetus to put his ambitious project into motion.

They had something that he had needed and, so far, they had delivered, even if it had been overkill.

Neutro dropped down and hooked onto her master's shoulder. Will whispered into her ear a single command: 'Prevent the advancing intruders to our burial site from reaching me and report back anything suspicious,' he said. She cawed in response and then took off to meet back up with Mono who was circling silently overhead. Neutro relayed the message with a burst of further caws and then they both disappeared from view in unison to the source of the motorbike sound in the distance.

Will readjusted the groaning body of Blake, who was slung lazily over his shoulder. 'You're not putting up much of a fight, now are you?' he said, looking to the lesion that was leaking blood from between the eyes of the funeral operative.

Blake was beyond saving. His body was torn to ribbons and his mind had been eaten away from his third eye, all that remained now was a semi-conscious human with no understanding of the concept of life, with a dormant disease that had been transfused into his very blood stream. A disease born from angels, one so powerful that the worst diseases that existed on Earth paled in comparison to what this could inflict on a human.

All Will needed now was to add another ingredient to Blake's disease and await a paired fusion reaction to create an unstoppable and deadly virus from being created.

Will thought that he had all the time in the world to carry out his plan. The idea had been festering inside him all the while that he had been restrained in Nate's body, before he could finally take control; sixteen years in the making.

He knew his power was limited on Earth and also

that with each passing day, it would diminish further.

The night at the church when he brandished his power had been overwhelming and foolish to use, as it now left him with little energy in reserve.

His original plan was thwarted by Stan on that night and it had surprised Will to learn that Ictus had helped Stan from behind the scenes.

Will was troubled that having Ictus, the angel of death, helping Stan was a bad omen and he couldn't fathom what Ictus' true purpose could be. There was more to this aloofness. Will shrugged off the thought and reasoned that it would not matter now if he succeeded in this quest. At least Stan and Ictus had now retreated from Nate's mind and the annoying, irksome scratching feeling from their presence had now subsided.

What really bothered him though was how Stan was still present on the Astral plain. By Will's reckoning, the casket containing Stan's ashes and the fireworks were all scattered to the four winds, so why was he still existing and not a wandering soul, lost to all eternity?

Will cast the thought aside and promised himself that he would send a message to Eosino later, to question the boy for information regarding his late father. Maybe Nate might have the answer, because Will was certain now that more of his father's ashes must exist.

Hurriedly Will pushed on, carrying Blake aloft, knowing that just up ahead and around the sweeping bend of the river lay his destination, a water treatment facility. The same one that he used to work at in his previous life.

His back-up plan was simple in design but difficult to implement in execution, it rested on a lot of luck. But the devil was in the details.

Blake's restrained body, covered in Stan's ashes, would attract two of Will's fallen angels to feast upon him, therefore transferring their otherworldly disease to pass from their saliva in bird form into his open wounds from their razor-sharp beaks as they opened him up and fed on his flesh.

Tibetans referred to this practice as celestial burial, where they would take the body of their deceased up a mountain and lay it to rest on a rock or *dakhma* as it was called. Carrion birds, or *dakini's* as they were known to Tibetans, would then arrive to devour the deceased.

Dakini, which translates to angels, come in the shape of the carrion birds that come and feast on the flesh of the body, which in turn would free the body's soul to heaven as an act of excarnation, thus taking the soul to the afterlife.

Will, having been a guardian angel himself once, knew only too well the different practices held by various religions and was always fascinated by one in particular, the Buddhist beliefs.

His own spin on it required the deceased to be alive though, and to stay alive, to allow the disease that the angels carried to spread into the blood stream, in turn making the victim a carrier of said afterlife disease. One that was far deadlier than any known on Earth.

Mono and Neutro had played their part, doing

just as Will had hoped, they even tore apart Blake's third eye, which is often referred to as the pineal gland, which would put him into a vegetative state so he would become pliable and not be able to be communicate to anyone what was going to happen.

Now that the disease was in Blake's bloodstream, Will just needed to add water to make it waterborne and that's where the water treatment facility came into it. The virus would be made and delivered into every household, via drinking water from every tap, in turn infecting 10,000 or so people, that would then infect a greater population whom would all die and therefore create a large army of souls for the afterlife. Will could then control and lead them to paradise to conquer for his own, leaving this pitiful existence on Earth behind.

All he needed to do was to bypass the water treatment security and the flocculant, sedimentation, filtration and disinfection stages of the facility.

Then it would be a matter of dumping Blake's infected body into the storage stage of the water process which would then allow the virus to become waterborne.

Blake's journey would then be complete, he would drown and rot. But as he wasn't aware anyway, Will figured it would be just fine.

'You almost ruined it for me Blake,' Will said, panting, nearing the facility and feeling elated at the prospect of amassing a large army.

'When you kicked me away, sending yourself strapped to the stretcher over the ravine, I really thought you were going to be a goner for sure,' Will said, slinging Blake's body to the ground.

'Then to find you still alive and cutting your bonds with that rusty old piece of metal embedded in the mud bank by the time I got to you, was a stroke of genius,' he added, slightly out of breath.

'I admire your resolve, I really do. I just want to say that I took no pleasure in watching my *Dakini* gorge themselves upon your flesh, I was just going to let them have a starter not a banquet, but you angered me when you kicked out and stunned me with your foot to my head,' he sighed.

'Still, if you don't make it, then I'm sure I can find a use for you in the afterlife,' he added, grabbing Blake by the ankle and dragging him off through a clump of bulrush that spread from the river onto land across his path.

Blake's ragdoll-like body smeared blood across the stems as he was dragged along, flattening the bulrush and tearing off their heads that released their cottony fluff from their innards.

'My angels should buy us some time so I can make my move up ahead,' he said, scanning the treatment's perimeter fence.

'All I need is an opportunity to present itself,' Will said, letting go of Blake's body.

'Whilst we wait I'm going to tell you a short story about a disgruntled employee, an unhappy guardian and a helpless prisoner that I think might make you feel differently about me, you'll see that I'm not a bad soul, I've just been dealt a shitty hand,' Will added, walking up to the fence.

The broken, bloodied and bruised body of Blake lay twitching on the floor. His mouth, which had been stitched up, now severed from when he tried to free himself earlier, allowed blood to escape down his cheeks that had been dripping down into his throat. All he could do was splutter between the frayed ends of the string that were pierced through his lips in a zig zag fashion.

Turning back to face the bloody mess of Blake, tied up and abandoned in the reeds, and with a gleam in his eye, Will said 'Anyway I digress. It all began about half a century ago...'

13

AVENGING ANGEL

Working as a water treatment facility operator, William Last was one of fifteen employees that worked in a gang of five over three rotating shift patterns, 24 hours a day, seven days a week and 365 days a year.

Taking the waste water from the Mala Sort river and treating it to make 10 million gallons of fresh drinking water every day, William Last started out happy in his career and felt pleased that he was making a difference to the citizens who benefited from the fresh drinking water they received from their taps in the nearby town and villages.

Unfortunately for Will, one fateful day whilst he was conducting routine maintenance on a sludge tank, he slipped and fell in when a hornet stung him upon the neck.

If it wasn't for a co-worker who was close by coming to his aid and pulling him from the tank, then Will would have drowned in human excrement.

After that day nothing would ever be the same again. William Last, who had got severe brain damage from the fall, had started to have episodes of paranoia and was convinced he could hear voices in his head. Unfit for work, he was discharged some weeks later on medical grounds and was told to attend regular meetings with a GP to under-go treatment to hopefully get fit again for work.

On one such visit to his Doctor, one morning he had an accident with a minibus full of children when he was distracted by the mysterious voice in his head.

Having only saved one child from a perilous fate, William Last had sacrificed himself in the process and drowned in the Mala Sort river, the very same river that gave him purpose in his job and had almost killed him at the plant many weeks before.

His last thoughts as he was swept away to his doom was how little anyone cared for him at work and how let down he felt by the lack of compassion and understanding they gave him following that incident, especially the jokes about him talking shit. Death to him in that instance felt like a massive relief.

But that too was short lived, for upon entering a world that existed between Earth and paradise as it was known, William Last was to be a Guardian Angel to the very child he had saved. The boy whose life he wished he could have avoided saving to have his own life back again.

Luckily for Will, the voice that he had been communicating with belonged to the one entity that could give him his wish, to have a chance at life again through an indirect course.

In a rather cunning twist, William Last had possessed the son of the child who had lived the life that he was robbed of and over the years, whilst waiting for the son to mature, Will had replayed scenarios over and over of what he would do when he finally had control over the boy's mind, *a la compos mentis*.

As William Last and the boy Nate exchanged personalities, a deep-rooted bond began to form. Over time the boy became to explicitly trust his inner voice of reasoning right up to the point when he was betrayed and banished to the confines of his own mind, overseen by the angels that Will controlled.

When William Last finally had full control of the boy, he knew immediately what he must do. Knowing that he could not take over the world of Earth, he set out to use his knowledge of matters that he did know from before, to take the world with him to the afterlife by using Nate as a bridge to the Astral Plain, to help him gain access with the might of an army created by him to overthrow the very creator of all things.

'So, this is where I find myself now, Blake. I am no longer William Last. He was weak and is now truly dead to me. I am now an Avenging Angel and I will have my revenge,' he said.

Just then a crow descended from the darkening sky just as night fell. Mono landed next to Blake's writing body and began to hop about cawing noisily.

'Thank you, Mono. Well that is very interesting indeed,' Will said.

So, my Anastasia has a glass pendant around her neck that sounds like it is singing. Could it be I wonder? Will thought, putting a finger to his top lip, lost deep in thought.

'Return to your sister Neutro and stall them but guide them here where I will be waiting for them with a surprise. It would seem that they have something I want after all,' he smiled.

Will made his way over to a large mesh gate set within the perimeter fence that had a 'No Trespassing' sign hanging on it and wedged an object into the mesh above the locked handle. He gave a smile to a CCTV camera suspended on a building within the compound facing him and then retreated back out of sight picking up a large rock from the grass verge.

14

GLASS HALF EMPTY

It was the start of another shift for Denny Bloom at the Mala Sort water treatment facility and already he was running late.

Having pulled on his blue overalls and donning his black wellingtons, he reached into his locker and retrieved his white hard hat, almost dragging out a plastic carton containing his *Waterzooi* with him. Catching it in the nick of time, he stowed his meal back into the locker and locked it shut.

Belgian-born, Denny was fluent in English but still found British cuisine lacking in taste. His mother had passed down her knowledge of traditional Belgian recipes that Denny still adhered to making to this day. *Waterzooi* was his favourite dish and he looked forward to eating it later.

Fastening his utility belt on, he then proceeded to check it contained all his essential tools. Happy he was all set, Denny plonked the hat on his head and made for the door, forgetting to turn on his hand-held radio.

Exiting the building, he grabbed a clipboard off a nearby hook by the door and took a bunch of keys from a nearby safe, he made for the office which was located a short distance away in an adjacent building, ready to go and collect the hourly data readings.

Night was beginning to fall, and the overhead flood lights began to flicker on as the timer began to click rotate.

No sooner had he made it half way across the path connecting the two buildings, when the office door opened and the concerned face of his boss peered out with a hand holding the inside handle.

'Den, before you start your shift, I need you to check the South perimeter gate. I just spotted a teenager on the camera go up to the gate and hang something on it. I can't quite make out what it is so I need you to check it out and report back to me what it is, okay?' he said bluntly.

Denny looked to the South side of the compound that was still in darkness, as it hadn't lit up yet from the floodlights which were on a different circuit. He pulled his torch from his belt, 'Yes, sure I will Boss. Probably some kids messing about. I'll tell them to sling their hook, shall I?'

'Yes, that's great Den. I'll have a flask of hot chocolate waiting for you by the time you get back,' he said, before closing the door.

Switching on his torchlight, Denny pointed the beam in the vicinity of the gate in the far distance and hurriedly made his way over, knowing it would take him at least ten minutes to get there.

By the time he had neared the gate, only half of the compound behind him was lit and he felt pessimistic for what he would find.

The water facilities moto was 'No matter what, we are a glass half full business'. But for Denny he was thinking totally the opposite right now as a shiver travelled up his spine.

He arced his torch across the gate and spotted something glistening at its centre. Tentatively he approached.

What he saw sickened him to his stomach. There, wet and dripping with blood, forced through one of the diamond shape holes in the fence was a severed tongue. Denny reeled away in horror.

He went to run and get as far away as possible when he then heard a plea for help.

He shone his torch down to the bottom of the gate and saw a man on the other side writhing around on the ground dressed in what seemed to be a funeral operative's attire. Denny fumbled at his belt and removed his radio, cursing that he hadn't turned it on already. He went to power it on then remembered it was dead. He had forgot to change the battery pack before he started his shift.

Putting the radio away, and in a blind panic, he grabbed a set of keys from his belt and found the tab for the South gate. He found the attached key and slammed it into the lock all the while keeping his torch beam trained on the moaning man in front of him.

Nudging the gate, Denny stole a look over his shoulder and prayed the floodlights would come on over this way already.

He pulled open the gate and dropped down by the man's side, shining the torch into his face, 'Are you okay? Can I help you?' he said.

But that was the last thing he could say, as a hand with a rock struck his hard hat with such force that his brain rattled in its cranium, making him dizzy and disorientated and sending the hard hat bouncing away into the reeds.

Trying to stagger to his feet, Denny saw three moving images of the same teenage boy approach him laughing hysterically, as he tried to back away.

'Help me? Please help me!' Will laughed.

As the three images slowly blurred into one, Denny tried to regain his composure and focus but the blood-spattered rock hurtled towards his eyes, sending him into a black void.

15

COLD SHOULDER

Heparin paced the length of the shoreline that spanned the outer edges of Petra's island, keeping to the sand that was exposed from the receding tide and avoiding the snow-covered inland.

Approaching an outcrop of rocks that peppered the break water, Heparin noticed two sets of footprints leading from the beach and out into a large cluster of trees.

Upon closer inspection he saw that one set of footprints had two snaking lines between them and knew instantly that his master's wings must have made them, as the tips would probably be dragging wet from his back.

He cast his glassy blue eyes back to the sea and thought that he had just caught a glimpse of some smooth grey flesh dipping below the waves.

Without hesitation, but feeling less brave than usual, Heparin decided to follow the tracks away from the bubbling sea where the island had now sunk from view to a safer environment where he felt more comfortable.

It didn't take long before Heparin found his master and the human, whom he wanted to savagely maim for poisoning him in his previous life, up ahead.

They were both sitting close to each other on a snow-covered log, huddled around a fire, in a remote corner of the island, sheltered on two sides by a high cliff face.

Not wanting to give away his position and still contemplating whether to punish this human called Dustin, Heparin circled closer.

Wanting to leap at the human unawares and drag him off into the woodlands was Heparin's plan, but for now he would abide his time whilst he waited for the right time to strike. So, he just sat on his hind legs and observed from a safe distance away.

His master and the traitor were engaged deep in conversation. 'I thought we had covered this already. Like I said before, you are well and truly dead. You are between Earth and paradise. I am Petra's deceased dad... and before you say anything, yes I know, I am an angel,' his master Nathaniel said, even though Heparin didn't understand their words.

'The cat you encountered belonged to Stan, you know. The cat you poisoned, Stan's cat! And yes you were the one who brought about Stan's untimely death, by bestowing him with that bloody comic, that I now find out from you that my daughter had retrieved from his artefacts from his dead belongings,' Nathaniel said exasperated.

Heparin caught a snowflake on his nose and licked it off as his tail swished behind him in the snow, aggravating his mood.

'Now you tell me she passed it onto my grandson Nate, your stepson... Brilliant, good job. You really are a piece of work you know that?' Nathaniel said, prodding the human and bringing his wings up over them both to shelter from the advancing snow.

His master sounded very annoyed and upset and Heparin wondered if he should just end the conversation now or not.

'What amazes me the most, is that you just confessed to being present when Stan unwrapped the gifted comic down by the river and you watched him from the roadside walk into the river in grief and did nothing. You went home and forgot about it,' Nathaniel said, beating the snow off that had collected across the surface of his wings.

Heparin decided to lick the snow that had settled on his fur.

'Oh, so you're sorry, you didn't realise that would happen. Well of course you didn't, how could you? I hope you have felt guilty ever since,' Nathaniel added, pulling away a wing from sheltering Dustin and leaving him exposed to the harsh elements.

Heparin was very keen of hearing, but he couldn't make out what the human was saying. He knew his master was scolding the human and sensed that the human was remorseful.

'I honestly don't know what to do with you. Clearly my daughter loves you. That was evident by how close your islands had converged and flourished. More so than when Stan was with her on Earth, but now she is without either of you and that pains me so, she must be going through hell and there is nothing I can do about it,' Nathaniel said gloomily, sliding further away from the human.

The human had been given what the angel referred to once as the cold shoulder. But Heparin still couldn't grasp the human language. He just read their reactions.

The snow began to fall harder, and Heparin found himself creeping closer to the heat from the fire.

'If you truly are Petra's soulmate then I don't know where that leaves poor Stan. It certainly is a predicament for sure,' Nathaniel said, standing up and warming his hands over the fire.

'There is much to discuss still, but for now I will leave you with your thoughts and I pray you find peace in all that you have done, God knows I can't,' he added, leaving the human alone, whilst he went off to find more firewood.

It was then that Heparin saw his golden opportunity, he would never forgive, nor would he ever forget what this human had done to him, not only had this human killed him, he had also separated him from his true owner, not the bird man but his human known as Stan.

Just inches now from the rear of the human who was facing away from him, shivering on the log, Heparin brought his front paws in and was ready to pounce at the human, when a black birdman came swooping in from the sky, causing a whiteout with its mighty wings and almost extinguishing the fire.

The human fell backwards from the log in fright and came face to face with Heparin, who couldn't believe his luck. Heparin hissed, then made a puffing sound with his throat. He knew his kind were not aggressive to humans, but this individual was fair game. He went to strike when a familiar voice boomed behind him.

Heparin turned and saw two figures emerging through the freezing fog, one was the birdman and the other was his human, his heart raced.

'Hello Hep, have you missed me?' came the voice that Heparin had been longing to hear.

In that instant, the snow leopard forgot about the puny human who cowered in the snow and bounded over to his old master to be reacquainted once more.

Heparin felt joy and elation; it was a feeling that he hadn't felt in a long time.

16

THE ONLOOKER

Rolling ice-chilled mist cascaded down the cliff-face like a silent and eerie waterfall, as if it was suppressing the mood in camp.

Dustin, cold, wet and miserable languished beside the fire and stared uneasily at the giant black angel who looked menacing against the backdrop of the snow-covered scenery.

Ictus gave the hapless human a piercing look and then looked away to the approaching party.

Following the angel of death's stare, Dustin caught sight of Stan and Nathaniel in the distance, he quickly looked away, burying his head in his hands.

Nathaniel stopped Stan in his tracks and put himself between Stan and the figures by the fireside, bringing up his wings to shield Stan from what awaited him there.

'We need to talk Stan,' Nathaniel said, grabbing hold of Stan's shoulders.

'Okay Nathaniel, but let's get to shelter first though, shall we?' Stan said, trying to pull the angel's wing down.

Nathaniel, knowing he was being observed from behind him in the distance, pulled a surprised Stan into a close embrace. 'No, not yet Stan. There are two things I need you to know before we get to camp, that cannot wait,' he whispered hurriedly, looking deep into the corner of Stan's eyes.

Stan, taken aback and now on edge, tried to break free. 'What is it Nathaniel that can't wait?' he said, trying to look past his father-in-law.

'Firstly, the company you keep Stan. Ictus is not helping you for your interests, there is much more you should know. Ictus is the Angel of Death, who, has allegiance to the powers that be, be careful that you are not a pawn in an agenda that you are not aware of,' he said with an affirming nod.

'Yeah, okay sure. But he has been a Godsend so far, Nathaniel,' Stan replied, pulling away.

'That's what concerns me,' Nathaniel said, as Heparin came trotting in between them.

'The other thing?' Stan said hastily, wanting to get to the warmth with his beloved cat who was now nuzzling against him.

'About that... Secondly, I need for your restraint, much has changed since you've been gone. You only have to see how cold and desolate my daughter's island has become in your absence,' Nathaniel said, building up to the point.

'Yes, I guess it has,' Stan said, looking around and now only realising that the landscape of his wife's mind had changed beyond all recognition since he was last here, years ago.

'There is no way to break this to you gently,' Nathaniel said, building up the courage.

Stan started to spin the tie that was wrapped around his wrist in frustration, 'Just tell me already!' he demanded, patience not being his strongest suit.

'Petra remarried soon after you died,' Nathaniel said, looking away. 'She took someone new into her life, someone you know,' he added, looking back to Stan for a reaction.

'I, I never really gave it much thought to be honest, I mean, I guess it would make sense. Our relationship was slipping away but I thought that it was just because I had my condition which pushed us apart,' Stan said, trying to come to terms with the revelation. 'I would never want her to be alone, we said that we would move on eventually if one of us died before the other, but I didn't really think it would happen,' he added.

'Well, happen it did Stan I'm afraid. You need to brace yourself for what I am going to say next,' Nathaniel said, puffing out his cheeks and releasing hot air into the cold.

'What is that?' Stan said licking his lips.

'My little daisy got together with… Dustin,' Nathaniel said warily.

'SHE DID WHAT?' Stan hollered. 'The creep who killed my beloved cat, the man who caused my seizure that put me here permanently, are you serious?' Stan said with anger boiling over.

'I am afraid so Stan, but there is more,' Nathaniel began to say, but Stan had heard enough and with his anger overflowing and his power building up, he cast Nathaniel aside like he was made of paper, sending the angel flying into a deep snow drift.

A slight gentle humming descended.

Stan stormed off with Heparin in tow and made for the fire that was struggling to stay alight against the falling snow.

Dustin, who had heard Stan's outburst, looked pleadingly to the black angel that resided over him. Ictus, expressionless, merely looked at Nathaniel who was trying to get back on his feet.

The onlooker beside the fire turned around and raised his hands in protest, 'Please Stan I'm sorry,' he said.

The humming sound grew more intently.

Stan came to an abrupt halt and tried to process who he was seeing. He blinked, trying to make sense of it all and sent power coursing through his veins that spread to his wrist, causing the tie to stiffen into a steel metal state. Brandishing the sword fashioned from his tie around his wrist, Stan screamed 'YOU!' before plunging head long at the mortified Dustin.

Ictus was swift and grabbed Dustin close into its arms and brought its wings up as a shield to a raging Stan. Stan rained blow after blow against the otherworldly metal feathers of Ictus' wings. Steel on steel, sparking wide to the sound of the repetitive humming that reverberated in Stan's thoughts.

'Damn you Ictus, give him to me,' he said, striking the wings with his makeshift sword again and again.

'His soul is not yours for the taking,' Ictus said,

with no emotion, from behind the barrier.

Stan dropped to his knees and laid both palms into the snow, where upon contact the crystalised snow began to rise up and solidify into icicles. Then with an uproar by an unseen force, the icicles snapped free, turned to face Ictus and like flying projectiles went whistling through the air with such velocity that they impacted across Ictus shielded wings.

Ictus, having sensed Stan's intentions, flexed the individual feathers of its sharp wings like hundreds of slicing scissors that obliterated the ballistic missiles into a showering cloud of fine dust.

'ENOUGH!' Ictus bellowed, 'Now is not the time, the pendant it sings for you Stan.'

Stan stopped and took stock of the heightened sensory humming that he had thought was a build-up of his rage and came to realise what Ictus meant.

Petra's daisy pendant that contained his ashes was calling to him from afar, as a faint signal emitting through the two plains of existence. The talisman was warning him, calling out to him to connect.

Stan put his fingers to his temples and bridged the connection. It was as if time stood still and he was bathed in an incandescent light that caused the falling snow to melt all around him on contact, as he transcended this plain to the one on Earth.

Slivers of distorted, blurred images tore away in his mind, peeling away into a black void to be replaced by another. He saw Arlo wielding a large sledgehammer and Ana close behind, running after him. Then he saw two crows circling the night sky above, giving chase. He felt like he was everywhere at once but nowhere in particular.

That image then peeled away to present another of a large collection of concrete buildings but was quickly replaced with the next vision of his son gloating over two bodies at his feet.

Stan tried hard to concentrate but the crows persisted in their pursuit. He heard them communicating to one another, they were making the noises that birds made, but beneath the facade came a whisper of a human language; *Harm them but don't kill them, Neutro. We must herd them to him.*

A searing white-hot flash of pain hit his senses and sent him reeling back to the Astral plain.

It didn't take him long to recover as he knelt there in a circle of waterlogged ground.

'Welcome back, Stan. What did you learn?' Ictus said.

'Ana has my only remaining ashes, Ictus, and she is being led into a trap!' Stan said rubbing his temples.

'I also saw two of the fallen angels, but they were birds. We have to act now whilst they are away from my boy,' Stan exclaimed, pushing aside the dull ache that now replaced the sharp stabbing sensation from before.

'We are not yet prepared Stan. Three still remain here. I must find a priest first to carry out an Adorcism for us. But in order for me to do so, I want you to promise me that you will do no harm to this individual whilst I am away,' Ictus said, gesturing to Dustin.

Stan, concerned for the welfare for his daughter and son-in-law and for the remaining ashes of himself, spoke flatly. 'Fine, but Dustin and I will have a very lengthy talk in the meantime, I can't promise Hep will be so patient though,' He added, watching Heparin being restrained by Nathaniel close by the fireside near to Dustin.

'I will let no harm come to him Ictus,' Nathaniel said, coolly eyeing the dishevelled human before him.

'Very well, then I shall return soon and explain what I have in store for William Last. I suggest you all find somewhere else to wait for me, as we cannot be granted safety in one place for too long. There is an ice-covered swamp a few miles inland from here that we should regroup at,' Ictus said lifting off.

Stan was reluctant to wait too long, but he knew he would make the most of this downtime. He looked forward to time with his majestic cat and to catch up with his father-in- law, but most importantly of all he was very curious as to why Dustin was now well and truly dead.

Dustin felt a rising panic set in as he regarded the party before him, wishing that the hideous black angel monster didn't have to go. The circumstances he found himself in were not comforting at all and he still thought that he would soon wake from this nightmare.

He wished that he could be an onlooker no more and return to the loving embrace of his dear Petra, the love of his life and his one true soulmate.

17

DEADWEIGHT

The party of four neared their destination without having had too much hinderance, Stan was out in front scouting the area with Heparin nearby, who was bounding off of exposed rocks through the deep snow drifts in a playful manner.

Dustin and Nathaniel lagged behind, trudging slowly and steadily through the fresh path that Stan had created.

Nathaniel desperately needed to calm the friction between his two sons-in-law but found Stan unwilling to talk further on the matters of the heart and Dustin had been difficult to coerce along, let alone even start a conversation.

Visibility had become poor as a recent thunder-snowstorm had descended, obscuring their vision with heavy snowfall and streaks of lightning in between each clap of thunder, temporarily blinding them with flashes of white light.

Stan, trying to keep tabs on his beloved Leopard, didn't notice the frozen swamp beneath his feet that was covered in a layer of loosely packed snow until it

THE OASIS OF LIFE

was too late. The ice cracked and he went down hard on his left knee as his right foot slipped through the glassy sheet causing him to curse out loud.

Nathaniel, momentarily disorientated by the strobe effects caused by the lightning streaks, shouted out in concern; 'Stan, are you okay?' he said, getting a mouth full of the persisting snow.

'Yeah I'm fine, I think we're here,' he said, pulling out a soggy foot from the frozen swamp, just as a slimy grey hand beneath the depths tried to grab him unawares.

Nathaniel and Dustin soon caught Stan up and blindly walked right into him, almost knocking him back into the freshly made hole within the ice, that had now broken apart. 'Careful, I don't fancy going in again,' Stan said in protest, turning to face them.

Nathaniel looked past him to the swamp and could just make out a faint outline around its misshapen edges, noticing it was broken up into smaller surrounding bogs, stretching out to the visible distance.

'I say we take shelter under my wings until this blows over, then look to collect firewood before we go any further, You know, in case one of us has another unfortunate accident,' Nathaniel said, flexing his charred tipped pinion's.

'No need, I have it covered,' Stan said, walking a short distance away and placing his hands to the snow at his feet to channel his power once again.

A large radius of snow beneath their feet began to hiss and melt away turning into a large expanse of water that then began to rise up to form a glacier wall around them. Then it began to arc rapidly above their heads, crackling as the ice formed a solid barrier, chasing the water that spilt over its newly formed edges.

'I'm impressed, I have to say, by the magnitude of your abilities,' Nathaniel said, scratching his bearded chin.

Stan looked at him wryly and gave a curt nod as Dustin cowered behind Nathaniel and watched in awe and terror of just how powerful his wife's late husband had become.

The ice wall continued to converge above their heads where it then fused together creating a domed roof, sealing over with a crack to form a see-through ceiling with Stalactites now hanging loose above their heads as they froze over the remaining drips.

Stan released his hands and admired his handywork when Nathaniel piped up; 'So, what about a door then Stan?' he smiled.

'Hmm, all in good time,' Stan said, turning his attention to the tie that had frosted over around his wrist. With a little concentration, Stan flicked off the ice and turned the tie into his ethereal sword once more. He then approached the wall in front of them, before going to work slicing out a large block of ice that he then swiftly kicked away to reveal an opening. 'That ought to suffice,' he added, feeling smug.

'Indeed, it wil,' Nathaniel said with admiration. 'I suppose we better call Nimodi over before he gets lost in this storm,' he added.

'Not this again Nathaniel. Look, I've told you before, his name is Heparin,' Stan said, poking his head through the ice doorway to look for his faithful companion.

'Okay Stan, I won't challenge you,' Nathaniel said, grinning, knowing that Stan was easily wound up.

Stan tutted then disappeared outside, calling out to the snowy Leopard. He scanned the immediate vicinity and wondered what his feline companion was up to. Suddenly the Leopard sprung from out of nowhere and bowled him over to then butt his face. Stan laughed and for an instant he felt content once more.

But it was to be short lived, when Dustin approached him from the side. 'Stan we really need to talk,' he said.

Heparin growled and came in between them, Stan, keeping his promise to Ictus, grabbed the cat by the scruff of the neck. 'It's all right boy, you will get a chance soon,' he said, restraining him and looking to his wife's new love with bitter hatred.

Dustin went to speak further when he suddenly clammed up with fear and pointed to the hole in the nearby iced-over swamp. 'What the hell is that?' he said, through his chattering teeth. Catching his gaze, Stan brought his sword up to his chest and took on an attack stance.

There peering back at them through the hole in the ice was a conjoining of grey, rotten slimy faces with a familiar face, head and shoulders above the others. 'That is Venous, or what is left of her and the grey matter,' Stan said amazed that she still existed.

'That thing tried to get me before Nathaniel showed up and rescued me,' Dustin said, backing away. 'What is it and what does it want?' Dustin asked.

'That, wife-stealer, is deadweight, just like you. I can allow it to take you which would not at all break my promise to Ictus,' Stan said, formulating a plan that Dustin would understand.

Just then Nathaniel appeared alongside them. 'No, Stan, you will not,' he said, then added 'That pitiful sight you see there Dustin is a collection of lost souls that are in purgatory, who roam the islands looking to create an army of the damned to swell their numbers. They are slaves to the evil that opposes us.'

The grey sinewy mass bobbed on the water line, staring back with cold unrelenting malice. Venous knew better than to take on her old nemesis, all she wanted was the human. So, with great regret, she gargled to the mass a simple command and they sunk from view leaving the party on guard and on edge.

'We best keep a sentry on duty at all times,' Stan said, then added, 'I personally think Dustin should take first watch, all in favour?'

'I will take first watch,' Nathaniel said looking at Stan with wry contempt.

'Whatever,' Stan said, leaving them to return to the shelter.

Dustin looked at Nathaniel with remorse and then decided to follow Stan into the shelter. Stan saw him approach. 'I suggest you look around for firewood,' Stan said, rubbing a palm around the smooth, cold interior of the dome.

Dustin went to move away then halted. 'Look, I don't want to be here anymore than you, I still don't believe that I'm...'

Dead? Well get used to it,' Stan said coldly.

'I'm sorry that I poisoned your cat, I really am.

But you killed my father,' Dustin said, pointing at him.

Stan clenched his fists, 'I did not kill your father, it was an accident caused by me, granted, I won't deny that. But it wasn't deliberate like the action you took. Besides, I was just a kid at the time.'

'I was a child too when I lost my dad. You will never understand a son's loss,' Dustin said, looking away.

Stan sighed heavily, 'Fine, I'm sorry that you lost you dad and I'm sorry that you felt that way but what I won't forgive is you marrying my wife,' Stan said, punching a hole in the wall of ice.

Dustin backed off to the doorway warily, 'I didn't set out to fall in love with Petra, it just happened. You weren't around anymore, and she needed company and support, I gave her that. It just happened gradually over time, it was never my intention, Stan,' Dustin said, keeping an eye on Nathaniel outside.

'Well she is still my wife first and foremost, so just you bloody well remember that, you hear me? When the time comes, I will collect her and together we will make the journey to paradise together as soulmates do, there will be no place for you,' Stan said, sealing over the hole he had created.

'What if she doesn't want to be with you, have you thought about that? What if I'm her soulmate? What then? Let's face it, you were never the perfect husband,' Dustin said, pushing out his chest in defiance.

Stan lost it to a rage that was building up within him and he saw red mist, extending his arms he pushed out against the walls of the dome and obliterated it into a thousand shards. Dustin covered his head with his arms and crouched down as he was showered in a blast of ice.

Nathaniel who had been petting Heparin outside and who was listening to the whole argument, raced over to Dustin's side to protect him.

Stan stormed up to his wife's second husband with his sword held high, 'Leave him be Nathaniel,' he said, spitting through his teeth. Nathaniel fanned his wings to create a barrier between them, 'I won't let you do that, Stan,' he said, shaking his head.

Stan went to attack, when out of the sky a dark winged figure fell from the heavens clutching another human.

Stan retracted his sword that had become a loose flapping tie around his wrist once more. 'Welcome back Ictus, I see you have found us a priest,' he said, noticing the dog collar.

Ictus landed in the middle of the feuding group, 'Did I miss anything?' the dark angel said, releasing the priest from its grasp.

Nathaniel eyed Stan cautiously, 'No, not at all. You couldn't have come at a better time,' he said.

'Good, then we have much to discuss,' Ictus said, then added 'Stan do you suppose you could make us shelter?' he added.

Nathaniel began to laugh which then spread to Stan, until at last, the ill-feeling had subsided once more.

18

BRAIN FREEZE

Petra found herself pulling on a cigarette in her car outside the mortuary chapel, whilst waiting for her youngest daughter Sally to arrive.

Sally, who had been trying to contact her mum in a blind panic, had found Petra's phone switched off and cursed that she could not get through to inform her mum that she was currently held up in traffic. She was sick with worry.

Petra, having forced herself to identify her late husband Dustin alone, had run from the mortuary in shock and jumped back into her car. The whole process had brought back so many mixed emotions, that it hit harder than the time before, when she had to do the same for Stan.

It had been so much worse this second time around. In fact, her love for Dustin had been so much stronger than her love for Stan, that she now found herself in a worse state than ever she had experienced.

Not being able to comprehend her current state of affairs, Petra's mind was numb and she felt frozen to the core as the reality of her situation began to sink in.

The night sky was getting blacker by the minute and she found her mood darkening with it. Her thoughts turned to Ana and Arlo and she hoped that they would soon find Nate safe and sound. She prayed with all her might that he was not at all involved and that everything would turn out okay.

How she wished to have her family around her in this time of need. They were now the only reason she had to hang on to life.

Petra's mind felt addled and it was as if she had brought about a brain-freeze as her grief took hold. Somehow, deep inside her mind and soul she could still feel Stan and Dustin giving her an inner strength to carry on but couldn't see a way forward.

Dabbing her cigarette against the wing mirror, Petra reached into the door-well and pulled out her phone.

She powered it on and waited for the mirrored screen to fade. Petra couldn't bring herself to go back into the hospital to see the Reverend Goole to make sure that he was okay, but now found she was wrestling with her guilt to return, then at least it would ease her burden.

The phone lit up the car's dark interior and presented her with an image of her and Dustin on their wedding day in a bland registry office, which was a far cry from the expensive one she had with Stan.

Quickly accessing her gallery, she found an old image of her and Stan and studied the strain on their faces, a far cry from the screen-saver of her and Dustin and happier times. Petra closed the screen and flipped to her contacts, searching for Ana's number in her recent call log. Tapping on the green phone symbol, Petra put the cell to her ear and pulled her cardigan tight around her bust and waited.

It wasn't long before an answer took place, but to Petra's surprise the call was ended abruptly, leaving her wondering what the hell was going on.

Feeling the need to reach out to her eldest daughter to get answers, and not happy with being hung up on, Petra hit the dial button again.

19

NIGHT TERRORS

The daisy pendant, containing her late father's ashes worn around Ana's neck, acted as a talisman warding off potential threats and bestowed her with a bubble of an unseen protection, the likes of which could not been seen or felt unless the carrier was in tune and focused.

Had Ana been spiritually in tune with the pendant, then she would have realised how much danger her and Arlo were actually in.

Going by the light of the waning gibbous moon above, Ana and Arlo had found themselves stumbling around in the dark looking for fresh tracks.

To add to their troubles, a pair of crows had attacked them on no less than three occasions. The first had been when Arlo had decided to stop and empty his bladder in the middle of a copse.

He was just zipping up when a crow dive-bombed his head and scratched at his face with its sharp talons. Ana had found it funny at first until a second crow had swooped down onto her shoulder and began to peck at her face. Luckily for her, the pendant had emitted an unseen power that caused the crow to retreat to the tree tops. Ana, screaming, fled along the river protecting her head in fright as Arlo made every effort to catch her up, swatting at the crow that was giving him grief.

By the time the pair were reunited, the two crows had taken to pursue them together, circling close above and shrieking intensely. Arlo, expecting another strike, had swung the sledgehammer in a high circle above his head but missed the targets wide, letting one of them sneak in with its talons extended to snatch at the pendant from around Petra's neck.

His wife grabbed hold of the chain and was yanking the pendant back as the bird was tugging it the opposite way above her head. Arlo could see the chain was biting into her chin as she struggled to hold on.

Grabbing hold of the sledgehammer with both hands, Arlo thrust it at the bird which made contact, causing the bird to release its grip and take flight to a nearby tree.

Eventually the couple were left alone until they found they had reached a high perimeter wired fence with an open gate at its centre.

Arlo spotted a white hard hat laid abandoned nearby and bent down to retrieve it. Holding it up to the night light he noticed that it had a large perforated hole in it with traces of blood around the edges. Puzzled, Arlo discarded it and approached the gate, noticing the glistening pink and bloody tongue wedged into the latticed wire gate.

Poking the severed tongue with his finger, and not quite realising what it really was, Arlo felt repulsed by the find and slowly pushed the gate inwards, beckoning Ana to join him. The tongue slipped from the hole and slithered down to the ground.

Ana, nodding in response, looked back one last time down to the river from where they came. She gazed around uneasily looking for the winged attackers whom had by now disappeared into the darkness of the woodland further down the line of the fence. With trepidation and fear from another attack, she hurried after him.

Feeling safe for now, husband and wife grabbed hold of each other's hands and made their way through the gate. But they were barely through when a loud moaning and groaning met their ears.

Arlo fearing the crows had returned, looked back to the foliage and saw to his surprise an unclothed man curled up in a cluster of stinging nettles.

Ana grabbed his arm and tugged at his jacket, 'No, don't,' she whispered, feeling like a bag of nerves.

'It will be fine, Ana,' Arlo said, placating her and making his way back to the man.

Feeling cold by the impending night chill and their ordeal, Ana looked on with worry as Arlo turned the gentleman over with hesitation. The semi-naked man was covered head to toe in nettle rashes and he had blood pumping profusely from his head. His body was streaked with mud and dried blood that had saturated into his underpants and socks at his feet.

Putting a hand up to her mouth in shock, Ana retreated backwards and slipped on the severed tongue in the dirt. Cursing, she collected her composure and kicked away the muscle into the undergrowth not clearly seeing it for what it was.

'We have to get help, darling,' she said, looking to the compound half-bathed in light to her left and darkness to her right.

Arlo, trying to get the man to his feet, looked to Ana and nodded as he hooked an arm around him. 'Thank you, the name's Denny,' the person said, standing shakily on his feet.

'I'm Arlo and that is my wife Ana,' Arlo said, steering the man around to face his wife. 'What the hell happened here?' he added.

'Can't... quite remember. Sorry,' Den said, gently stroking the wound at his head and wincing in pain.

'Don't worry, we will take care of you. Is there somewhere safe we can take you?' Arlo said worryingly at the state of the battered human before him.

Denny Bloom pointed to the office nestled between the flocculant and sedimentation buildings; 'Over there,' he said, before slumping in Arlo's arms. Arlo hoisted him to his feet and hooked the sledgehammer under Denny's arm 'To use as a crutch,' Arlo said, receiving a nod of approval from the disorientated water treatment employee.

Ana went to help stabilise Den as they ventured into the compound, when a voice shouted out from the darkness, 'Hi sis, were you looking for me by any chance?'

Arlo shot Ana a worried look, 'Don't even think about it,' he said, as if reading his wife's mind.

'Too late,' she said 'Get that poor man to the office and call for help, I'm going to sort my brother out,' she added, with anger rising within.

Knowing better than to argue with his wife, Arlo replied 'Fine, but be careful,' he added with pleading eyes.

Ana gave him a kiss on the cheek, 'You know me,' she replied, before turning away to catch sight of her brother once more.

William Last, acting as the wayward brother, raised his hands to the darkness and summoned his servants in the guise of the two crows from beyond the perimeter, just as Ana treaded carefully towards his direction in the black of the night. She watched them swoop over the fence and perch on each of his wrists, sending a cold chill up her spine.

'Say hello to Mono and Neutro,' Will said, throwing the crows to the sky, then switching on his torch. He swung the beam around and into Ana's face, causing her to stumble.

Blinded by the light, Ana raised a hand to block it out, 'What the hell have you done, Nate?' she said, trying to look through her fingers, then added 'When I get a hold of you, then you will be well and truly screwed,' she said, advancing once more and avoiding the shaft of light.

Clad in Denny Bloom's work attire Will looked to the ladder that ran up the side of the clear-well storage tower and could just make out the silhouette of Blake's body resting on the concrete roof.

'You've got to catch me first,' he said in a child-like tone, as he whipped the torch around to locate Ana.

Ana, briefly illuminated, ducked away back to the darkness again and kept pushing forward, risking a quick glance over her shoulder to see Arlo dragging Denny away to the dimly lit office in the distance.

'Find and stop her by any means necessary,' Will shouted from behind the torch, as he wildly swung it about looking for Ana.

The crows Mono and Neutro cawed in unison as they scoured the night sky looking for their prey below, unlike owls, their vision in the night was poor at best and they had to rely on the beam from the torch to show them the way.

Will caught Ana in his sights causing her to step left into the shadows again. He arced the beam to the right and caught her again. 'There she is!' he screamed, as he made for the ladder and began to climb up, still swinging the torch to his side.

The crows advanced on her position and almost collided mid-flight as they came at her from two different trajectories.

But still Ana pushed on with steely determination and scorn for her brother, as she danced around the sweeping beam.

Arlo dragged Denny Bloom along and could hear the commotion at his rear, all he wanted was to get this man to safety and call for help. Then he could assist his wife, who he felt was in serious danger. She loved her brother deep down, that he knew. But Arlo also knew how malicious and vindictive Nate could be.

Denny Bloom, who was still dazed and confused, squinted at the dancing light that moved up the side of the building. *He's giving away his position, the idiot* he thought.

Ana tried her best to avoid the night terrors that brushed past her face in the darkness. But they scratched away her skin with their sharp talons and beaks as she wandered in to their paths unwittingly.

Eventually, she sidled up to the side of the clear-well storage tower and saw the metal wrought iron ladder snaking up its exterior, the light was sweeping wide away from her last known position and she knew now that she had to be quiet to get to the top safely.

The crows screamed maddeningly in and out of the darting light and Ana was glad to have avoided them mostly so far.

Steadily she climbed the ladder and felt the cold steel of wrungs in her palms. She was barely half way up when her phone vibrated into life with an upbeat melody.

Ana almost fell from the ladder in fright as she fought with one free hand to silence her phone and to keep the other gripped to the wrung. She had just silenced the phone, when the light beam snaked past her and lit up the building opposite her direction, signalling the advancement of the shrieking birds.

The moon converged behind some passing clouds and granted her some well-needed cover in the dark that it left behind.

Thinking that she was safe for now, Ana continued to climb the ladder until she finally reached the top. She poked her head over the edge and felt thankful that she had not been spotted by her brother who was still focused on shining the torch away from her, scanning the adjacent building.

THE OASIS OF LIFE

Will was standing close to an open trapdoor with a circular mechanical handle, that sunk hinged into the concrete roof. Below the exposed door was ten million gallons of pure drinking water that was slowly being distributed to thousands of homes that spanned the length of a football pitch.

Between himself and the crumpled body of Blake, who was laying bloodied and unconscious, lay the open trapdoor to the clear-well.

Having pulled herself up and onto the roof, Ana stood up and gently stepped toward the shadow of her brother against the skyline, not aware of the obstacles in her way.

She had just made six steps when her phone vibrated into life once more, accompanied by her melodious ringtone. This time the beam of light swung right round to meet her and flashed in her face. The second call from Petra carried to ring on through the silent night.

The fallen angels Mono and Neutro screamed towards Ana's face with their talons spread out. Ana went to rush to her brother when suddenly she tripped over the body of Blake and fell headlong into the icy water of the clear-well storage tank below.

Will, chuckling now, walked over to the opening of the clear-well and shone his torch in. The shaft of light lit up the water that had an emerald green tinge from the lights aligned in its inner walls.

'All too easy,' Will said, as he watched a lifeless Ana in the water below float to the surface, then added 'I think you could do with some company down there, sis,' he said, dragging over Blake's dying body and kicking him unceremoniously into the hold with her with a splash.

Shutting the hatch with a heavy clunk and turning the wheel shut, Will smiled inwards as the crows landed on the steel door and tapped the door with their beaks.

Will laughed into the night sky, as the compound's remaining floodlights came on and bathed him in their fluorescent light.

'All good things come to those who wait,' he said, knowing that on contact, the infected body of Blake would contaminate the clear-well storage water and Ana as well.

20

ADORCISM

Stan felt an icy dread wash over him as the pendant containing his ashes, that was around Ana's neck, came into contact with the water in the clear-well storage tank back on Earth.

With his eyes shut tight back in the Astral plain, he tried to focus on Ana, fearing that something bad had happened to her, but all that he could sense was panic and isolation, then the vision and feelings passed leaving a searing pain behind his eyes.

When Stan opened his eyes again, he saw Ictus huddled in front of the group inside his freshly made shelter with the Reverend Goole at the dark angel's side.

Nathaniel, who sat directly opposite Ictus with Dustin to his left and Stan now petting a bored Heparin to his right, having clearly just experienced something that made him look tense, sensed that he could cut the atmosphere with a knife from his two sons-in-law frosty behaviour.

The Reverend Goole had been instructed by Ictus to explain what an Adorcism meant and how it would factor in to the proceedings. 'So, an Adorcism is quite the opposite from an exorcism, whereas the latter casts an evil soul out from the host, leaving the host free from their burden, an Adorcism places the rightful soul back into their body which in turn will force the evil entity back out.'

'I've never heard of such a practice,' Stan said, feeling agitated and looking distant, wondering what the priest made of the daunting predicament he now found himself in and if he felt terrified, like him, with not being able to do anything about it.

'It's very rare indeed,' the priest said, snapping Stan out of his trance. 'There is not much call for it these days for obvious reasons,' the priest added, trying to work out if he was dead, in purgatory or both, having had his faith well and truly tested.

'Okay, so how does it work exactly" Stan said, shaking off the dazed spell. 'I mean, I don't see you carrying a bible, a cross and some holy water, or is there something I'm missing?' Stan said with urgency, stroking a finger between Heparin's eyes.

The Reverend regarded the group for a while and then sighed heavily, 'There are four stages to the act, step one requires the righteous text to be read aloud by a priest, the second requires holy water to be splashed upon the host, the third requires that the two souls acknowledge and accept their fate in the eyes of the Lord. For the fourth, a godly spirit is required with a pure heart to swap the two souls around by using extraction and insertion.'

Nathaniel, who had been deep in thought up until now, suddenly made a contribution to the conversation and addressed Ictus; 'We're surrounded by snow and ice that we can melt down to bottle and bless for the holy water. We also have an abundance of pure angels at our disposal for the exchange and I'm guessing Father Goole can carry out the Adorcism to the letter. So that just leaves the issue of getting Nate and Will to accept they are who they're supposed to be and not what they have become,' he concluded.

'I'm afraid there's just one deed that you may have trouble with,' the priest said, shifting closer to the doorway.

'Like what exactly?' Nathaniel replied.

'Well, like the fact that you need a priest to be able to recite the words fluently and I'm sorry to say this, but I cannot be that person. I for one don't have the words on me to recite anyway, I would also have a hard time remembering them, as my mind is not what it once was. Secondly, none of this can be real so I choose not to offer my help and I will control my own dreams,' he said, bolting for the opening.

'Seriously Ictus, I thought you said he had accepted his fate?' Stan said, springing to his feet.

Ictus shot out a hand to restrain Stan, 'Give him a minute to come to terms with his purpose. You see he is not dead, he is undergoing a heart bypass back on Earth as we speak. The priest is very old after all and has witnessed some strange events that a man of the cloth would have trouble coming to terms with his faith upon seeing,' the dark angel said.

'No, we don't have time for this, I fear for my son's sanity and my daughter's life, we have to act now whilst there are only two fallen angels holding my son captive and whilst Ana is in great peril,' Stan said. But before he could act, Dustin raced for the doorway, 'I'll go, he might listen to me,' he said, disappearing into the frozen landscape.

Stan, looking astonished at what he was witnessing, looked back at Nathaniel before dashing after Dustin with Heparin following close behind.

Nathaniel rose to his feet slowly and looked to Ictus, 'I should go help too before something happens to either of them,' he said, casually strolling out of the shelter.

The storm was fading to the distance and the snow was falling gently by the time Nathaniel caught up with Stan, who was gazing upon the frozen swamp to the two figures of Dustin and the Vicar engaged in a heated discussion in the middle of the ice-covered bog. Dustin was trying to drag the priest off the ice whilst pointing down at their feet.

Before Stan could shout out a warning about its stability and what Dustin was referring too, the ice cracked below the figures feet and Dustin fell through it, grabbing hold of the Priest in the process and dragging them both down below the surface of the water.

Nathaniel beat his wings and took off in flight, signalling to Stan to stay back as he glided across the frozen marsh. Stan watched the spectacle unfold as Heparin and Ictus joined his side.

The Vicar bobbed to the surface first as Nathaniel swooped over his head and snatched him up into his arms where he then circled back and let the screaming priest drop down into the soft snow drift at Stan's feet.

Ictus stooped down and retrieved the Priest from the snow pulling him close into its arms. 'Perfect. You're right, Stan, we have lost too much time already and too much danger surrounds us. We must leave now for Nate's island before it's too late and we get unwelcome attention,' it said, lifting off with the mortified Priest in tow.

'But, but what about Nathaniel?' Stan stammered, watching his father-in-law heading back out to the location of Dustin who was struggling in the icy depths with a grey mass of flesh that had joined him.

'That is not our immediate concern, we leave now. I suggest you leave your cat here if you are worried for their safety,' Ictus said, turning away to the sky.

Stan looked to Ictus and then to Nathaniel who had dived head first into the throng with a giant splash, tearing up the ice. He didn't know whether he was coming or going. Hesitating, Stan said 'Hep, I need you to stay here, boy, alright? Protect them,' he added, grabbing hold of Heparin's mane and nuzzling the big cat's nose with his own. 'I won't be long,' he said, releasing his grip and walking away, leaving the Leopard to wonder just what the hell had taken place.

Stan felt bad for leaving Nathaniel and Heparin again but gave no thought to Dustin's safety at all. He swept some snow off an overhanging tree branch and followed the direction of Ictus and the priest, crunching the snow tight into his palm as he focused his power and turned it into a hard ball of ice. 'We're going to need this I guess,' he said, as he approached the tree line and looked back with guilt before he disappeared into the thicket and out onto the coast, watching Ictus sail across the vast expanse of sea to his son's island on the horizon.

Sometime later, standing at the water's edge, Stan flicked out the tie from his wrist that in turn solidified into his makeshift sword. He then jabbed the sword into the ground where, upon contact, landmass began to surface from below the waves, creating a narrow pathway that spread outwards between the two islands as a makeshift bridge, with relative ease.

Stan, heavy with a guilty conscious, then stepped out onto the path with Nathaniel words haunting his mind *Beware of Ictus, the angel of death. Be careful of hidden agendas.*

Pulling his collar up tight around his neck and then retracting his sword by using the power of his mind, Stan turned it back into its material state, where the tie then flapped noisily from the wind blowing across the beach.

Then he crossed his arms and continued his journey with his head hung low to avoid the spray from the sea as it crashed into the sides of the pathway. Stan made his way across in trepidation upon spotting tendrils of seaweed criss-crossing the path as it made him wary of the dangers the sea held.

If I only I could rewind time and start again, then maybe I would still have my darling wife, I hope that Dustin gets his just desserts, it will do me a favour if he is no more, Stan thought darkly, as he dispersed sand from under his feet and broke into a run.

21

MEMORY RETRIEVAL

The grey, monstrous rotting flesh of Venous conjoined with her cohorts, pulled Dustin through the freezing cold water beneath the ice-encrusted surface.

Nathaniel swam after them using his wings to propel him along at great velocity as he gave chase, drilling through the water and struggling to hold his breath. He had never given it much thought up until now of what would happen if he drowned whilst already being dead but figured that the lost souls whom he chased would result in his fate if it was to happen.

He also couldn't risk the fate of his second son-in-law becoming one of them too as he had made a promise to his daughter Petra a long time ago that he would always protect her husband whilst he was in the Astral plain, granted she had meant Stan at the time, but circumstances had changed and Nathaniel still upheld his views that it meant her current husband, which just so happened to be Dustin at this current time.

The last thing anyone deserved after death was to become a lost soul wandering from island to island, retrieving and consuming other lost souls with an never-ending appetite for all eternity, to take humanities lost memories and fuse them with their own because they had lost their way and purpose to reach paradise.

Nathaniel was damned if Dustin was to become just another memory retrieval. Petra would need someone to collect her when she passed over or she could succumb herself to becoming one of these sad and lonely lost souls. There was no way Nathaniel would allow that to happen to his precious Daisy, *she will go to paradise* he thought, as he neared his quarry.

Heparin, who had been watching intently up until now in the shadows streaking below the ice, suddenly found himself missing Stan and so made his way back to his master's frozen shelter to have a well-deserved sleep away from all the commotion.

Just when Nathaniel thought that he would either run out of air or not catch up to Venous and Dustin, something unexpected happen. From all around to his front and from the sides, appeared barb-tipped spears that penetrated the ice creating shafts of light that lit up the gloomy depths with a loud sound of ice breaking in every direction.

Distracted by the spectacle, Nathaniel ended up swimming right into a now motionless Venous, who had stopped swimming as she tried to figure out what was occurring much to the dismay of her mindless posse who were still fixed trying to make Dustin one of their own.

But before either could react, a large net which was attached to each of the spear handles quickly chased the spears descent and both parties underwater now found themselves tangled up in the meshwork that enveloped them as they reacted too slowly to back away.

In an instance Nathaniel, Dustin and the collective of Venous were all suddenly hauled from the water via the net and out onto the snow-covered land by a large mass of angels that had surrounded the entire radius of the swamp.

Nathaniel went to speak when the angels who had quickly retrieved their spears, closed the circle around them, and began to thrust their spears into the throng of the hideous twisted bodies and limbs of Venous and her grey matter causing a deafening screaming and wailing as the mass was swiftly executed.

Iyanla, the dark-skinned angel who had an affinity with Nathaniel, reached down and cut a large hole in the net for him and Dustin to squeeze through. 'You can't be left alone for one moment without getting yourself into trouble, can you Nathaniel?' she said.

Happy to see her, Nathaniel smiled; 'You know me,' he replied, twisting his wings to free himself. 'Is this horrific monster destroyed then?' he asked, kicking at a protruding arm.

'Unquestionably! So, anything else you would like me to deal with for you?' Iyanla said, flicking blood off her spear and unwinding it from the net.

'Yes, actually there is. I need an army to come with me to my grandson's island, like now. We have to help Stan,' Nathaniel said, grabbing a hold of her shoulder.

'No need, I despatched an army earlier when Ictus telepathically sent word, so you can relax for a while,' she replied.

Nathaniel looked at her nervously then he looked to the skies. *I hope Stan heeds my warning, there's something not quite right about all of this,* he thought.

'I must go too, Iyanla, I fear Stan is being misled by Ictus. The angel of death was the main reason I escaped paradise,' Nathaniel said, looking at Dustin who was struggling to escape the net. Then he added 'The methods employed to tip the scales of the almighty war to our favour by harvesting innocent souls is wrong and unjust.'

'Please don't pursue this,' Iyanla said.

'You know it's wrong. To strengthen our numbers and overthrow our adversaries by using innocents is not our way. I must aid Stan and warn him of such matters,' Nathaniel said, extending out his charred wings.

Iyanla snapped her fingers and the other Angels joined her side. 'I wish you hadn't said that Nathaniel, for we must fight fire with fire,' she said, shaking her head.

'What? What do you mean?' Nathaniel replied, feeling hemmed in.

'You can't let it rest can you? So, you leave me no choice. Why can't you just accept some things are better left alone and unsaid, why do you have to make things so damn difficult for yourself and others?' Iyanla said, prodding her spear into his chest.

'I don't understand…' Nathaniel said, looking to the grave faces circling him.

Iyanla sighed, 'I'm so sorry Nathaniel, I truly am

but you leave me no choice,' she said, snapping her fingers once more.

Two angels from behind Nathaniel brought their spears down in unison, slicing off his wings from his back, Nathaniel fell to his knees to join his wings as they landed in the snow beside him, coating the white snow in crimson blood. Nathaniel mouthed the word 'Why?' as the remaining angels stuck their spears into his torso and twisted them clockwise.

Iyanla approached the fallen angel with tears in her eyes, 'Ictus has found a way to end this war for all eternity and the plan must go ahead for it to succeed, again I'm sorry, brother, but your sacrifice to allow thousands more to join us is the only way,' she said, blowing him a kiss, then turning away, 'I will miss you,' she added not wanting to look.

'Iyanla, no…' Nathaniel pleaded.

'Do it,' she said, closing her eyes.

An angel stepped up beside her with his spear horizontal to his shoulder and nodded her way, before swinging the sharp end towards Nathaniel's neck.

Iyanla heard his head land in the snow. 'Bury his body, but bring me his head,' she said, without looking back and approaching Dustin who was struck dumbfounded. 'You will not speak of this matter, or you will share the same fate, do you understand?' she said, regarding him coolly.

Dustin nodded and looked away from the carnage in front of him, he felt that he had awoken into his own personal hell.

22

CLEARWELL

Ana heard a body splash into the water above her, followed by the hatch being slammed shut. She opened her eyes and looked around the wide expansive tomb of clean drinking water that she now found herself in.

Green neon lights covered in wire mesh embedded into the steel walls, two feet apart, spread around the tank's interior on all four sides, giving the water its luminescent colour.

Swimming to the surface, she was met with only an inch gap of air between the surface of the water and the tanks ceiling. Treading water and sucking in large lungsful of air, Ana saw the body floating not far away and swam over to it, livid with her brother's actions and shocked to the core of what he was capable of.

Scared senseless, Ana grabbed hold of the floating body and turned it over, hoping that the person was alive and well. But a lifeless man's face swung round to greet her and the look of torment from his dead eyes made her blood curdle. A name badge came away from his coat revealing him to be Blake Grant, a man that worked with her stepfather.

In a blind panic, Ana pushed the body away in disgust and reeled in terror, looking for a way out, only to find the closed hatch as the only point of exit.

Ana made for the hatch, hoping that Arlo would come to the rescue in the meantime, as she tried turning the round metal handle on the hatch, but the position of herself in relation to the hatch above proved too much of an effort to turn and she found herself quickly becoming weak.

With one last effort she tried again to release the wheel but overcome with exhaustion, her fingers slipped from the cold hard steel handle and she sank back down into the clear water.

*

'God damn it man, what do you mean the telephone line is dead?' Arlo said impatiently, holding a cold compress to the head of Denny, the water facility worker.

The water treatment facility manager, Tony, looked across to Arlo and Denny from his desk and put the phone down, 'Like I said, it's not giving me a tone. Look, look at the window of the CCTV camera, screen four. The telegraph pole in the background there is sparking. I'm guessing it's been tampered with,' he said.

'Well okay then, I get it, you don't own a mobile phone which I find very strange indeed, but someone must have one, Denny do you have one?' Arlo said, looking into the shaken man's eyes.

Denny, wrapped up in a blanket and shivering, said through chattered teeth 'It was in my overalls that were taken from me, sorry.'

'What about you? Don't you have one?' Tony said, bringing a cup of hot chocolate over for Denny and looking wide eyed at Arlo.

'Shit, yes you're right I do,' Arlo said, digging around in his jacket pocket. 'With all that had happened, I wasn't thinking straight.'

Arlo pulled out his phone and dialled the police, 'Here you go Tony, tell them what I told you okay? I need to get to my wife,' he said, removing the compress from Denny's head and getting Denny to take over. 'Can I borrow a radio to contact you on?' He added, spotting a recharging dock with two radios in the slots.

'Hi, yes I would like to report a crime,' Tony said, before he was interrupted; 'Sure, by all means Arlo, channel nine will give you access straight to me,' he said, then added 'No sorry, officer not you, sorry hold on one second,' Tony said, covering the mouthpiece. 'Please, if you find my other workers then tell them to come directly back to me, I'm really worried for their safety,' he added, turning back to the phone.

Arlo nodded and snatched up a radio, checking it was on the correct channel, 'Denny, Den, screen 11 camera is overlooking the place where my wife disappeared isn't it?' he said, jabbing a finger at the monitor.

'Yes, that's the one where your brother was last? That is the clear-well storage tank, that he was standing atop of when the lights came on up on the roof a little while ago,' Den said, trying to shake the image from his mind.

'Great then that's where I'm heading.'

'Yes definitely, you should go there, but be careful,' Den said, dabbing the compress around his eyes.

Arlo gave him a smile, 'Nate is the one who should be careful, because I'm going to kill him when I catch him,' he said, opening the door from the office and retrieving the sledgehammer that was propped up against the wall to the right of the doorway.

Tony, who had just finished his phone call and had hung up by the time Arlo made it to the door, went to tell him something when one of the many monitors on his desk sounded an alarm, causing an overhead light to start flashing red. 'What now?' he said, tapping away on the keyboard and bringing a message front and centre on the screen.

Arlo halted at the door with sledgehammer in hand and looked to the two men's faces 'What is it?' he said.

Denny looked from the screen to Arlo, 'It says the clear-well storage tank has been contaminated, Tony can we bring the camera up looking into the storage tank?' he said, looking gravely to his boss.

Tony swivelled his chair and turned a knob to cycle through the camera's and clicked the knob in when he settled on the camera he wanted, bringing the image into full size. 'What the hell is that in the water?' he said, straining for a better look.

Arlo recognised instantly what it was, 'Not what Tony, but who? Oh God, it's my wife. Shit, my wife's in the water!' he said, fleeing for the door.

Denny called after him, 'Be bloody careful!' he shouted, then turned to his boss 'Tony we have to purge the tank and stop the water getting out.'

'Already on it, Den, I just hope we catch it in time,' he said with grave concern. 'If you're up for it, I may need you too.'

*

Stan had only got a third of the way across the raised sea bed when the vision washed over him again, causing him to stumble mid run and forcing him to his knees.

'No not now, I can't be too late,' he said, as a loose connection to the pendant took hold once more.

Everything however became clearer this time, as Stan saw William Last parading around in the skin of his son, on the roof of a large concrete building, mocking whatever it was below his feet from a circular hatch.

He then saw his son-in-law Arlo calling out to Ana with fear in his voice, passing by a darkened room where two workmen were being feasted on by two crows. Stan put his fingers to his temples and looked deep inside himself until at last, he settled on an image of the pendant. He then took full control of his ashes within the daisy pendant that was around Ana's neck. Immediately, he felt his daughter succumbing to the watery grave that she was sinking into and knew he must act. The fear of losing a daughter coupled with a father's love, coursed through his very soul and out into the pendant as he manipulated his ashes imprisoned deep within, causing the atoms inside it to alight.

The ashes began to fuse together inside the glass, creating a red-hot blistering mass, heating the sealed pendant in the process. With much concentrated effort, the pendant exploded outwards and sent a shockwave through the water, shattering the pendant and forcing Ana to slam into the wall as the water pressure increased and ripped the overhead hatch from its hinges, sending it flying like a frisbee into the night sky and enveloping Ana in a stream of hot bubbles.

Stan felt Ana regain her senses and for a brief moment, father and daughter had become one, where each other's thoughts and feelings were transferred between their minds in a sudden rush of still-like images. But just as quickly had the images manifested, they soon subsided as Stan's remaining ashes on Earth disintegrated into the water, leaving him with a cold harsh dread that the water could be tainted and that soon a great population of life on Earth could perish.

Ana had felt it too, as the embers of her father's ashes diminished leaving her with no doubt that he had come to rescue her from beyond the grave. It was as if she was granted exclusive access to the afterlife and to answers that great scientists could only imagine attaining. Feeling that a great cleansing had absorbed into her very being, she knew that she was safe from the virus that had spread through the entire clear-well tank, which would run out into the homes of the innocent people that would drink it unawares and die from a horrible death, resulting in a mass genocide.

Swimming for the open hatch, Ana felt elated that she had experienced a rare, special once-in-a-lifetime, bittersweet moment with her dad and she began to tremble and cry.

By the time she pulled herself out through the

opening and to freedom, she knew that her dear brother was being controlled by an evil soul called Will, gleaned from the shared experience with her father. She knew now she had to help her dad from this end to send Will back and bring her brother Nate home, regardless of the circumstances he may find himself in on his return.

Ana rolled onto her side and deeply exhaled, dispersing water from her lungs as she coughed and spluttered onto the coarse surface of the tanks roof, all fight had gone from her.

A figure came rushing up to her and she heard metal hitting the concrete beside her as a familiar voice spoke to her, 'Ana thank God you're okay,' Arlo said, sitting down beside her and cradling her in his arms. 'I was so worried,' he added, brushing her wet hair from her forehead.

'So you should be,' a voice said, from behind them.

'Nate, you little shit, you wait till I get hold of you,' Arlo said, reaching out to get the sledgehammer he had thrown to the ground only moments earlier.

'You looking for this, brother?' Will said, holding the sledgehammer aloft and spinning it around playfully.

Ana grabbed hold of her husband's lapel, 'No, Arlo don't. That's not Nate,' she said, but it was too late. Arlo had let her slip from his side and was fast approaching his brother-in-law, overcome with a temper of hatred inside, 'You better hit me good with that, or else I'm going to hurt you so much that you'll wish you were never born,' he said, squaring up to Will.

'Too late, I already regret that! But my work is

done now so give it all you've got Arlo, if you think you can take me,' Will said, mockingly as he backed up to the roof's edge and stole a look below.

Arlo bit his bottom lip in anger and made his hands into fists, slowly approaching Will.

The two crows that had been busy earlier feasting on the two dead workers, now flew up and over the building's ridge where they settled once more onto Will's shoulders with flesh hanging from their beaks.

Arlo stopped and begun to back away, 'Shit,' he said, as the birds came flying in his direction.

'I never said it would be easy for you, brother, but once I'm done with you both then you can leave this place… in a body bag,' Will said with a big grin on his face.

23

DEPLETING CELLS

Stan carried on with the rest of the journey with his sword once more brandished, idly slicing away at the tendrils that were hindering his path and choking the pathway as he sought to comprehend what had just taken place.

The shared experience with Ana earlier weighed heavy on his mind, in one hand it was good to have insight into her history in that brief moment of the times when he was not around, but in another it pained him to witness her loss of growing up without him. His biggest fear however was regret, for although he had saved her life, he now knew that there was nothing else he could do to aid her as all connection to Earth was now beyond his control. He hoped that Arlo would get to her in time.

One thing he was sure of however, was that Ana now had the knowledge to see through Will's disguise and maybe she and Arlo could help bring Nate back from his ordeal in limbo, if the Reverend and Ictus were to succeed on this side of the veil.

Nearing the island of his son's mind, Stan looked upon the approaching barren landscape with sorrow to the bare twisted trees that loomed high above him. They seemed, to Stan, to mirror his own state of mind and just how bigger the task they had still to climb. He had lost Ictus and the priest when the visions had come, but he had a good idea of where they were heading.

He felt the ball of ice melting in his hand and focused his power once more to give it a frosted coating *I'm going to need this soon,* he thought, as he slipped it in his pocket.

Stan loitered at the tree line and readied his sword, expecting the two angels that had his son captive to announce themselves to him. It was far too quiet, but what troubled him more was just how elusive Ictus had been and how quick the angel of death was to abandon Nathaniel in his time of need.

Pushing his way through the trees, Stan felt the oppressive mood bearing down on him with Nathaniel's warning still toying with his emotions.

His thoughts quickly turned to his nemesis, William Last.

So now William is victorious in amassing a great army from thousands of souls by poisoning the well. So that means, in order to bring them over to the Astral plain he would surely be gearing up for his next insane plan, which must be to march on through to paradise for his own gains. But in order to do so would mean that Will would need to end his life on earth to lead them....

Stan started to piece it all together ... *which would rob Nate of returning to his own body and that would mean Nate would become... a lost soul! Oh God, I must hurry.*

Stan's pace quickened as he raced through the

desolate waste-ground, trying not to give away his position as he clambered over felled trees and across the multicoloured leaves strewn around.

Could it be that Ictus had planned this all along? For Will to have an army of his own creation that Ictus could use to balance the war for good and not for Will's intentions? Stan pondered, making his way to where he believed Ictus and the priest had landed.

Stan pushed on and eventually came to a small clearing where he was presented with a large Black Lotus structure at the heart of the glade. 'So nice of you to join us, Stan. We would have waited but unfortunately, they are observing us,' Ictus said, boring the words directly into Stan's mind with telepathy.

It didn't take long for Stan to figure out that it was Ictus in a protective state which meant the priest must be with the deathly angel safe inside, which was quickly confirmed when Stan heard the priest reciting the holy scripture of his Adorcism from inside the cocoon.

With trepidation, Stan crept closer and listened to the words that were amplified from within the shell. 'Father, I ask you in the name of all that's pure and good to send out angels to gather up the fragments of Nate's soul and restore him into his rightful place,' the Reverend Goole said aloud.

Stan heard the wind whip up through the trees ahead, sending the kaleidoscopic colour of leaves spiralling upwards and creating a howling maelstrom which was then accompanied by the three angels known as Baso, Lymph and Eosino, who glided gracefully out into view as if by request.

'You can't,' Baso said, shimmering.

'You musn't,' Eosino added, with her arms outstretched.

'You won't,' Lymph said, wagging a finger before joining hands with her sisters, trying to prise them away.

Reverend Goole, who could not see them but could hear them, became flustered and agitated as he tried to peer out from his confined space.

'Focussssss!' Ictus hissed, drawing the priest back to the task in hand.

'With, with the full power and authority, I ask the angels to unearth and break all earthen vessels, bonds or bindings which have been put upon Nathan Palmer's soul by any means,' the priest added, quivering.

The angels drifted over to the closed black lotus structure like moths drawn to a flame, as Stan gave them a wide berth, scouring for his missing son.

'I thought the angels had to be pure of soul?' Stan said aloud, backing away from the mesmerised angels.

Ictus, hearing his words, formed a mind link, 'They are Stan, it's just that they are controlled right now, so we need to give them back their free will and restore order, to do so requires great effort, but to do so ensures that we erase their very existence, if this doesn't get a reaction from Will then we are lost.'

Stan watched the angels circle Ictus and try to probe the exterior for weakness.

'Is there anything I can do to help?' Stan said, cradling the iced ball in his pocket and eyeing the angels circling around Ictus, with their palms outstretched and their fingers touching the angel of death's feather incisor wings.

'No, but be patient Stan, this will all be over soon,' Ictus replied.

'Okay, you deal with that then, I'm going for Nate,' Stan said, breaking for the direction that the angels first entered.

'No Stan, not yet. It's too early, we need the remaining angels and William if we are to fully succeed, this will deal with our current predicament but not the bigger picture, I don't want you jeopardising this by getting yourself in trouble if they appear to you when I can't protect you,' Ictus said, spinning on the spot as the priest began to falter.

'Keep going,' Ictus said to the Reverend, who was struggling to carry on with his rite. Stan took that as being aimed at him, 'Okay I will,' he said, then added 'I have to see my son... I miss him!'

'Not you Stan, Father Goole, Stan don't...' Ictus said, but Stan had gone.

Ictus extended the sharp feathers outwards in anger, 'Continue Reverend,' it added.

'Hmm,' the priest grumbled, then said 'Restore all the pieces of Nathan's fragmented mind, his will and emotions. His appetite, intellect, heart and personality. Bring them all into proper and original positions where they belong.'

Disappearing into the wooded area, Stan heard the priest's words fading behind him.

I must get to Nate now whilst those two angels are engaged and the others are still on Earth. I can't let him down like I have Ana, I won't, he thought, trying not to give away his position.

Stan travelled onwards until at last he came to a large oak tree that had been hit by a storm. It had been cleft in two by a lightning bolt and was stood isolated with white feathers coating the bark up and down its trunk and all around its protruding roots at its base. Stan was about to skirt around it when he caught sight of a figure huddled high above in a blackened-out hollow.

Far from the view of the oak tree, the priest, under instruction from Ictus, was battling the angels with the final stage of his holy scripture.

'I ask you angels to break, cut and sever all fetters, bands, chains, ties and bonds of whatever the enemy has placed upon Nathan Palmer's mind by word or deed,' he said, ending his recital.

Baso, Eosino and Lymph tried to resist the lure of the priest's words and the pull of Ictus' power but were subservient against their will, as they wrapped their wings around the angel of death's Lotus form. Ictus, sensing victory, increased his pivotal momentum and shot out his razor feathers, impaling the angels to the carousel, until at last the angels were spun around in a blinding blur.

Baso, Eosino and Lymph wailed with distress as their forms were slowly absorbed into Ictus very fabric of being, like white cells depleting from view into a dark invading mass under a microscope.

Stan heard Ictus again in his thoughts, 'It is done, but be warned for a retribution.'

Stan shook off the warning and regarded the tree,

it had been a long time ago since he had climbed one but now he found himself starting to scale its branches with ease, until at last, his gaze drew level with the frightened form of his long lost son.

'Nate, is that you?' he said aghast, not ever having met an adult version of his son.

24

ENGRAM

Stan sat atop the bough of the tree and had his hand placed on Nate's knee for comfort. Nate, squirming, pushed himself further back into the hollow with his knees brought up into his chest.

'It's alright now son, I'm here to look out for you. I swear no harm will come to you whilst I am around,' Stan said, inching closer.

Nate looked at him with tears rolling down his eyes and Stan felt awash with love for his son who looked frightened, vulnerable and afraid.

'Do you remember me?' Stan said, feeling himself well up inside.

Nate wiped the tears away with a snuffle, 'I have photos of you bouncing me on your knee and a comic that you owned when you were a boy,' he said, letting his knees drop down.

'Then you must know that I am here for you now?' Stan replied, taken aback that Dustin had passed on the comic to his son in order to worm his way in to his affections.

'Dad, what is this place? I don't like it here. I want

to go home now,' Nate said, taking hold of his dad's hand.

Stan wanted to burst out crying but knew that he had to be strong for the both of them. 'Soon son, I promise. There are things that I must explain first,' he said, ruffling the boy's hair soothingly. 'You're so much like your mother, I can see you have her heart too,' Stan added, drawing his hand away.

It was hard to believe that his boy had all grown up but was still so vulnerable even if he was now a teenager. Stan prayed that would never change.

'Where are we, dad? Is this all in my head?' Nate said, squirming out of the hollow.

Stan swung his legs over the bough and patted it for Nate to join him. 'This may be hard for you to hear Nate, but you must believe in me. This island that we inhabit is the manifestation of your mind that exists between Earth and heaven. It is a place that you visit when you are near death or have died, an Astral plain that all souls inhabit when they eventually die, ready to cross over to the other side, whether that is paradise or Hell. As far as the eye can see beyond your island, lies other islands that belong to millions of souls like yourself, like I once was,' Stan said, looking for understanding in his son's eyes.

Nate looked around and exhaled, 'But I haven't died, have I? And why are you still here, if you have?'

Stan wondered if his son could handle the truth of what he was going to say next; 'Okay, look, you're not dead. You are just a prisoner in your own mind. Your body has been hijacked by an evil man called William Last, who is using you as a vessel to collect a large gathering of souls on Earth to bring here to overthrow paradise,' Stan stated.

Nate sat there in silence mulling over what he was just told before he decided to put an arm around Stan's waist and speak, 'I know him, he was my imaginary friend who told me awful things when I was young, but I thought he was just that, imaginary. I thought it was all make-believe, dad.'

'Come on, let's get down from here shall we?' Stan said, turning around to find a foothold below.

Nate watched him descend and then called after him, 'You still haven't said why you're here?'

Stan stopped midway and looked up to Nate, 'I'm here to right my wrongs. You're here because I made some selfish decisions when I was alive, if I had listened to your mother then maybe we wouldn't be in this mess now and I wouldn't have had a premature death... come on son, follow me,' Stan said, feeling regret.

'So, are you stuck here then' Nate said, hanging from the bough.

'Until I find a way to send you home and deal with Will, then yeah I guess I am. Maybe then, when the time comes as it does for us all, I can collect your mum when she finally passes, and we can leave for paradise together,' Stan said wistfully.

Nate started his descent and watched Stan leap to the floor, disturbing the feathers and then dusting himself down. 'You do know mum remarried, don't you?' he said, working his way down.

Stan looked up at Nate then turned his back on

him, 'I am aware she moved on with Dustin but that doesn't matter now. I'm Petra's true soul companion and that's all that counts. Why did you feel the need to tell me that, Nate?' Stan said, holding out his arms for his son to jump into.

Nate shook his head, 'I can do it alone, thanks,' he said, ignoring the question and leaping down to the ground.

'This way,' Stan said upset, still feeling stung by Nate's question and by how calm his son was.

'So, exactly how do you suppose you're going to send me home and get Will back here?' Nate said, walking close by.

Stan stepped over a felled tree and decided to sit down upon it. 'We have a plan in motion, but it is very dangerous, my being here alone put's us all in great peril,' Stan said, taking a moment.

Climbing over the tree and sitting down beside him, Nate looked at Stan and decided to probe further, still not really believing all this was real. 'How so? Those three angels goaded me and said you would come and fail,' he said.

'Those angels that held you captive are your white blood cells within your body and their purpose is to eradicate any foreign bodies from entering. To them, I am that threat. I only exist here as a memory trace, buried deep within you from your memories of me. Your mum had a name for such a thing, she called it an Engram I think, which I guess is what I am now, it's funny what information you retain.'

'But the two are unrelated, so how does that work?' Nate asked.

'I shouldn't exist here is the connection. Your mum is a very skilled physician in her field, I'm sure if she was here, even she would have a hard time getting her head round it. You see, when William Last took control of you, he meddled with an unnatural force and now everything is out of balance.'

Stan patted Nate on the shoulder, 'I always admired your mum's work,' Stan said, lost deep in thought. 'I still miss her you know; I love your mum very much. I love you all,' Stan added, getting back onto his feet.

'So, if I'm not dead then, does it mean I'm near death?' Nate said, catching Stan off guard.

Stan turned and faced Nate, 'Not if we force Will back here and return you home, it won't. Besides, all the bad things that have happened to you and what you have been through were not actions of your own doing, only Will's. He will pay for his mistakes, not you.'

'So, I won't go to Hell when I, you know… eventually die?' Nate said, wanting to never return to this foreboding place.

'No. Not if I have my way. I just don't know what will become of you back on Earth with the desolation that Will has left behind for you take the blame for. I'm afraid some things I cannot undo and are beyond my control, especially now,' Stan said with remorse. 'I'm sorry Nate, but I feel my time is surely coming to an end, I just wish that we could have longer together,' Stan added regrettably.

'That's alright dad, with all that has happened to me and if this is all real, then I believe in you. If this is just my mind playing tricks on me then I'm glad I have conjured you up,' Nate said, smiling. 'It means I must be getting better.'

Nate rushed over and gave Stan a hug, Stan embraced him. 'Oh son. I admire your resilience. You have made me one very proud father,' he said, giving in to his emotions as the tears flowed.

Stan was more than happy to have shared and bonded with the son who he was denied of seeing grow up, and in that special moment he thanked the Gods for giving him one last chance of redemption with his long-lost son.

'I'm so glad we shared this time, dad. For the record, you're a much better father than Dusty. It's a shame I will have to let him raise me instead of you,' Nate said letting go, not at all fazed by the strange circumstances he now found himself in.

Stan reached out and held onto Nate's shoulders, as he found himself fighting with his emotions. *Nate doesn't know about Dustin, how stupid of me to think otherwise, whilst he is trapped here, he is oblivious to what's been happening back home. How the hell I do approach him on this?* Stan thought.

'What's the matter, dad?' Nate said, snapping Stan from his dark thoughts, 'What is it?' he added.

'Nothing, son. I'm just happy is all,' Stan lied, reasoning that some things were best left unsaid.

Father and son regarded each other for a moment, before Stan suggested that they should return together to meet up with Ictus and Reverend Goole who would be anxiously awaiting them.

As the pair walked side by side, Nate shared stories of his upbringing and Stan listened intently to every word his son said, feeling giddy and almost complete once more.

By the time they joined Ictus and the Priest, Stan realised that they were now joined by a dozen of angels that were at the beck and call of Ictus.

'I see you have brought in reinforcements,' Stan said, approaching the group, then added 'Everyone, I would like to introduce my son Nate. Nate, that weird thing there is Ictus with Father Goole shielded from us, I'm afraid I don't know who these angels are though, so you will have to forgive me. I don't see Nathaniel though. Ictus, where is he? I would love for him to meet his grandson,' Stan said, looking around.

A dark-skinned female angel stepped forward with a bloodied sack and threw it in Stan's direction. The sack hit the floor with a squelch and rolled between Stan's legs where a severed head fell out at his feet.

Stan recoiled in horror, shielding Nate's eyes as the dead stare of his father-in-law's face stared back at him.

'Oh my God, Nathaniel!' he said dumbstruck.

Stan, in disbelief, collapsed in shock, his mind whirring with questions, wondering what cruel fate had in store for them now.

25

THE OASIS OF LIFE

Diving out of the way of one of the crows that swooped past his head, Arlo narrowly missed the opening of the clear-well storage tank as he landed, and barrel-rolled away to safety.

Will, who was watching eagerly from the edge of the roof, felt a sharp stabbing sensation behind his eyes and tried to shake the feeling away as he commanded the crows to shapeshift back into their original forms, 'Enough of this, finish off these annoying mortals now!' he yelled.

Too weak to help her husband, Ana pleaded with Will to let them go, but it only fuelled his ego. 'Don't worry big sister, when this is all over and I return home, I will be sure to trade your souls as I lead us victorious into paradise,' he said, rubbing the pain away from his forehead.

Ana rolled onto her stomach and tried to push herself up, 'Let's get one thing straight you maniac,' she said, pushing up with all her might, 'I am not your big sister, William Last. My brother is trapped inside you and will soon come home when the ritual is complete, leaving you to be just a figment of his imagination,' she laughed, pulling herself up onto her unsteady legs.

'What are you talking about? How do you know my name? What ritual?' Will said, shining the torch into her face, 'Answer me, bitch!' He demanded.

Ana, grabbing her knees to stabilise herself, looked at Will like a crazy woman possessed. 'Fat chance, psycho,' she cackled.

Mono and Neutro, having retreated to the sky above, shimmered from the light of the moon. They began to metamorphose, with their wings stretching out to their sides and their beaks started shrinking, as their humanoid, angelic appearance took hold, shedding white feathers and sending them spiralling downwards.

Arlo joined Ana at her side and took her hand in his, more for his own benefit than hers. He watched the angels above materialise and found his grip tightening, 'I have no idea what the hell is happening darling, but I won't back down,' he said, looking at her affectionately, as drifting feathers sank down out of sight to the clear-well below.

Will, furious that he was being defied, shouted to his fallen angels to attack. Mono and Neutro, hearing their master's command, swooped down and each picked out their chosen target.

Mono struck first by lifting Arlo off his feet and wrapping her wings around him as she buried her sharp nails into his flesh at his chest.

Neutro, knowing that Ana was weak, swooped down and swatted Ana off her feet with a swoop of her wing.

Will dropped the sledgehammer to his side and circled the hole above the clear-well storage tank, hoping that the virus was already being pumped into thousands of homes. He looked into the tainted green water and saw the decomposing body of Blake floating beneath the surface and smiled.

'It's funny don't you think? That water is the giver of life and without it we all die. It amazes me that we rely on facilities like this to provide fresh drinking water and we don't ever question what chemicals that they mix with it to provide a clean service,' Will said, before spitting into the well.

'This storage tank which holds millions of gallons of water is like an Oasis of Life, supplying water to plants to nourish and grow for human sustenance, whilst providing animals and humans with the basic need for survival. It's always fascinated me how easily it is to contaminate too, that could reverse the effect on life, that humans take for granted daily... so here we are,' Will said, watching Ana and Arlo fighting for their lives.

The sharp pain throbbed and pulsed behind Will's eyes again and he closed them to the pain. The vision filtered down through his mind and showed him Nate with Stan by his side, followed by a quick flash of a dozen angels gathered around father and son in a circle with Ictus and a priest in the background. Then he saw faint remains of his fallen angels splattered around Ictus shell.

Will came back around with his eyes wide in terror, feeling emptiness where fulfillment should be. 'No! No, no, no. I will not have my plan ruined now. Mono, Neutro, leave them and return to the Astral plain immediately, I can finish off here before I depart, protect my investment. Go now!' he hollered.

Immediately the angels let go of their fearful prey and twirled up into the night sky like ballet dancers pirouetting, screaming like banshees.

Will, still reeling from his vision, looked to Ana and Arlo who were both violently shaking beneath him. 'Once I'm done with you, I will break Nathan's body upon the hard concrete below,' he said, as he went to retrieve his sledgehammer.

Spinning around though, he noticed it had been removed. Then, from out of nowhere, a blunt force from the hammer hit him square in the back of the head, inflicting trauma from the cold hard steel of the sledgehammer that had been swung by Denny Bloom, who was now fully clothed and had crept up behind Will unawares.

'What in all that is holy, were they?' Denny said, watching Will's crumpled body splayed out before him.

Ana and Arlo slowly returned to their senses, as Denny pulled the radio from Arlo's belt and held down the trigger to talk, 'You were supposed to keep the comms. open,' he said to Arlo, then 'Tony, it's me. Both Arlo and his wife are safe, although a little shaken. As for the teenager, he is taken care of. Any chance I could have a raise? Over.'

The static on the other end crackled in to life, 'Seriously, no. But that's marvelous news Den, keep the boy restrained, the police are on their way. Whilst you're at it, check the water balance. The computers going ape shit over here, I couldn't purge it from the control room, the system tells me it's not bloody air tight now. Can you shut the hatch so we can purge the tank and shut it off from public access?'

Denny peered into the tank and saw a bloated body floating at the surface, he pulled the trigger again. 'I don't think so, boss. I don't know how to put this, but, you see the hatch is missing and there's a dead body in the tank,' he said, releasing the trigger.

'Then I can confirm our worst fears, Den. In fact, I think we are going to have to manually shut it off, over.'

Denny pulled the trigger on the radio again, but this time words had failed him as he stood there in deathly silence.

*

'Why Ictus? Why did you allow this to happen? Nathaniel was always loyal to you,' Stan said, covering the head over with the bloodied sack.

'Was he? Then why did he leave paradise? He could have served us an eternity but instead he wanted another chance of life. His selfishness was his undoing, he could have prevented this event from coming to fruition,'

'Rubbish! He was right about you then? You want an army of innocents for yourself,' Stan said, looking around and feeling outnumbered from all the angels that had surrounded him and Nate, 'You let him escape thinking he had a choice so you could kickstart your revolution'.

'Better that I have the army to protect your precious paradise then have an easily led fool like

William Last think he can wield an army against us, don't you think?'

'But why at all Ictus?' Stan said, weighing up his options.

'Because Stan, I am the angel of death. I set all the plans in motion from the offset. Who do you think was behind Will and Nathaniel's decision making?'

'I've come to realise that now,' Stan spluttered. 'But why would you use them like pawns?'

'You are all my pawns, as you so elegantly put it, Stan. Evil has spread throughout and is running rife across the Astral plain, tilting the balance against us in its favour. I was tasked with evening the odds or tilting it back. I simply chose the latter,'

'Well I think that these innocent souls that are about to come flooding into the plain should have a choice whether to fight your eternal struggle or not,' Stan said, solidifying the tie into steel at his wrist.

'That is why I chose you, Stan. I gave you your powers. You are the grey to the black and white. It was you that has made all this possible and you have not disappointed me. But if you so wish to do what I think you will do next, then that is your prerogative. But know this, think about your son, your daughters and your wife's future. When they succumb to death like all souls do, will you be looking out for them to escort over to paradise? If it falls and evil reigns supreme then what eternal misery awaits them and the rest of your kind? Think about it.'

Stan pushed Ictus words from his mind, trying to block the angel of death having access to his true intentions, 'Why should I step back and let you dictate our fate?'

'Because Stan, it has already started. Look, Will has sent his guests ahead already,' Ictus said, gently spinning on the spot.

Stan looked past the crowd of angels in front of him and saw Mono and Neutro drift into view.

The dozen angels, led by Iyanla, turned to face their fallen sisters and with a war cry, Iyanla led the charge to attack them.

Stan, shielding Nate behind him with his sword outstretched, watched the scene unfold.

The battle was brutal and swift. Neutro was there one minute and gone the next, blending herself into Iyanla, taking control of the leader's movements. She spun Iyanla with her spear in hand and slayed three angels that had frozen with fear.

Mono lifted off and gracefully glided over to a group of four angels in her path, wrapping her wings around them, ensnaring them as one, where she absorbed their spirits with contact alone. The four angels withered like dying plants under a scorching sun, dispersing into a cloud of ash.

One of the remaining four angels screamed out, 'Ictus, please help us!' he said, then added 'They can consume us by touch alone if they wish. You must help!'

But it was too late as no answer came, and the angel was skewered through the midriff by Iyanla's spear, then pulled into Neutro's clutches where he was devoured.

Mono cornered the remaining three angels who

stood their ground, remaining loyal to Ictus, as Neutro exited Iyanla's body, leaving behind her empty husk that fell to the ground, sending up a plume of ash in its wake.

Ictus, spinning wildly now, spoke directly into Stan's mind once again, 'Pawns Stan, don't you see? It's not too late for you, accept your fate or risk a punishment if you disobey me. Either way you cannot win this one.'

Stan hesitated and stood transfixed by the spectacle unfolding as Neutro and Mono morphed into one entity creating an angel with four wings and two heads.

The remaining angels beat their wings and flew towards their advancing enemy in a winged formation but were knocked back to the ground by an unseen force of wind created by the beating of the newly conjoined fallen angel's wings.

Then it was all over as the four-winged, distorted angel was upon them feasting upon them with both its ravenous' mouths.

Stan turned to Nate, 'Whatever happens, son, know that I love you very much,' he said.

Nate looked at his dad, imploring him to stay, 'Please dad, don't.'

Stan felt tears running down his face as he turned his back to his son and made for the unholy creation ahead. Raising his sword, Stan went to swipe when it turned back into the cotton material of the flimsy tie.

'I don't think so,' Ictus said, again invading Stan's mind.

Stan looked at his wrist in disbelief to the tie laying limp as the chanting of the priest from within ictus protective state met his ears.

'Dad, help!' Nate shouted from behind him as the ground gave away at his feet.

Stan turned in shock.

The ground split open and swallowed Nate whole, taking him from view.

Stan stared on with disbelief, 'What the fu...'

'And now your son has returned home. Last chance Stan,' Ictus said directly this time, over the priest's familiar words.

Dropping to his knees and planting both palms to the ground, Stan vented his rage and went to channel his power through the dirt to create a vortex, but nothing happened.

'Have all your abilities gone too? That is a shame. So, what are you going to do now Stan?' Ictus said with mirth.

26

WHERE THERE'S A WILL

Sirens wailed in the distance, accompanied by the fast approaching red and blue flashing lights of the local police enforcement.

Ana and Arlo were slowly regaining their strength, huddled together watching over the unconscious and twitching body of Nate.

Denny Bloom was pacing up and down, agitated, having just returned from shutting the water feed off. 'So you expect me to believe that the water has been infected with a catastrophic virus created from those, those things, that I saw disappear, which I am led to believe are angels, is that correct?'

Ana shivered against Arlo, trying to steal some of his body heat, 'Yes, that's exactly what I'm saying. I just hope that you have stopped it in the nick of time.'

Denny looked at her worryingly, 'If what you have said is true, then I seriously hope so.'

Arlo brushed away Ana's wet bedraggled hair, 'So what do we do with Nate then?' he said, watching the boy's body convulse.

'If my father has succeeded and Nate returns as

himself, then his soul will have been saved... but at a considerable cost, if not then we cannot let him take his own life or it will have disastrous consequences'.

'What cost are you referring to?' Denny said, watching the lights drawing closer.

'He has desecrated my father's ashes, mutilated and killed Blake and assaulted you, not to mention killing our step-father. There is no getting away from the severity of that,' Ana said, watching her brother slowly recover.

Denny caught her eye and stood over Nate's body with the hammer ready in his hand. 'Don't forget that he has almost drowned you, his own sister and killed two of my co-workers and probably even wiped out half the population of the village nearby by now.'

'That is harder to prove though isn't it? I will say I fell in to the tank trying to rescue Blake. Your co-workers were attacked by birds and the virus is a new strain which, like most viruses, has no known origin. They can't pin those on my brother.'

'What about these so-called angels I saw, how do we explain them?' Denny said.

'We don't. Besides who would believe us? They would lock us all up for being insane,' Arlo said, rubbing Ana's back.

'That's it, Arlo. You're a genius,' Ana said, giving him a peck on the lips.

'What? I don't...'

'We prove Nate insane. That way he can avoid prison and be taken care of in an institute, we owe it to him.'

'I'm having a hard job believing you, but okay, I trust your judgement,' Arlo said, putting his coat around her.

The boy's eyes opened and he groaned, lifting a hand to his head.

'Nate. Is that you?' Ana said, crawling over to him wearily.

The teenage boy slowly sat up and looked around, 'Mmm, where am I? What the hell is this place? Aren't we supposed to spread dad's ashes tonight or something? Or did I miss something?'

Ana pulled him in close and gave him a hug. 'There is much we have to talk about little brother and we don't have a lot of time. Do you trust me?' She said relieved, convinced it was her brother.

Nate looked at Ana with a loving affection, 'Yeah, sure I do sis. I know I have been a right pain but, but I think I'm broken somehow…' He said as the sirens drew closer, 'And I'm scared.'

Ana cried on hearing his words, 'That's alright, Nate. I promise you that we will be here for you all the way, we will get through this together, I promise.'

*

The priest, held up inside the protective clutch of Ictus, was instructed to call an end to his ritual, which infuriated a vulnerable Stan, who had now become the target of the monstrous fallen angel that was Mono and Neutro combined.

Stan scrambled over to Ictus and began banging his fists onto the dark angel's steel-winged shell, 'Damn you Ictus. You've made your point!' he yelled.

'Not yet I haven't,' Ictus said, moving away like a spinning top to reveal the pool of water beneath. The same pool that Ictus had placed the strange object into when Stan and Ictus had first visited here.

The four-winged and two-headed angel drifted silently over to a defenceless Stan and was almost upon him, when a large geyser of water erupted from the pool and deposited a surprised and furious William Last into their midst.

Will quickly got a reading of his predicament and commanded Mono and Neutro to attack Stan, puzzled by their combined form. But they didn't obey as they approached him as one, 'Attack Stan you fools!' he yelled, slowly backing away.

Stan shouted from behind Ictus' carousel form, 'They won't do that Will, you're as much a target as I am. Who's the fool now hey?'

Will felt that something was wrong and didn't feel right but couldn't put his finger on it, 'Where's your little Nate, Stan? You can't hide him from me forever. Or do you have him with you Ictus?'

'Nate's returned to where he belongs Will, surely you must sense that?' Ictus said, opening up slightly.

Will spun around and brought his palms up to his face. 'No this isn't right; Nate should be dead. Only then can I sacrifice his lost soul here and now to my fallen angels Mono and Neutro, then I can make my escape and collect my army.'

Stan, feeling more loathing for Will than for Ictus, remembered the ice ball inside his pocket that had begun to melt and caused his side to freeze. He took the opportunity, pulled it out and lobbed it into a small opening in Ictus' shell, 'Bless this Father, I have a plan,' Stan said, drawing the two-headed angel towards him.

Ictus read Stan's mind and nodded, 'Don't you mean my army Will? I guess you weren't killed in Nates body on Earth, such a shame for you,' Ictus said, blocking the four-winged angel from getting to a forlorn Will for now.

Stan skirted around to the back of Ictus and received the ball back as an arm extended the offering from the priest within, 'It is done,' the Reverend said.

Will opened his eyes just as Ictus backed away. Stan took aim and threw the iced ball at him where it exploded on contact with his face. Momentarily stunned and taken by surprise, Will went to wash it off when Stan followed up by pushing Will into the oncoming path of the spliced monstrosity.

A horrified Will, who had not yet adjusted to the realisation, was quickly taken aback as four wings enveloped him. Stan watched as his nemesis Will had the jagged teeth of Mono and Neutro open wide and clamp down on either side of his neck, spraying arterial blood as they feasted hungrily upon his tainted soul.

'Accept your fate Will, repent!' Ictus shouted, 'Then and only then will your torment end,' he added.

William Last screamed in anguish, 'Okay, I repent damn you, I accept my fate, let me go!' he wailed, knowing it was over.

On hearing his words, the blending of the two angels merged with Will and exploded outwards, snuffing his existence and separated the angels back into their original selves, but they were still apparitions.

Feeling bittersweet that Will was no more, but fearful that he too might suffer a similar fate, Stan looked for an escape route. *Did I really just get extremely lucky?* he thought, making his mind up and spotting a route.

He went to leap across the pool of water, when from below the surface emerged four tendrils that shot out and wound around his arms and legs bringing him onto his backside into the pool with a large splash.

Trying frantically to urgently free himself, the tendrils sensed his struggle and wound tighter around his limbs. 'Give me a break!' he shouted.

'Mono and Neutro cannot touch you now, gatekeeper. The Adorcism is complete,' Ictus said, boring his words into Stan's mind.

The tendrils stretched Stan upwards and pulled him in opposite directions, displaying him like a star perched upon a Christmas tree. 'Gatekeeper?'

'What the hell are you doing?' Stan said, watching the two angels circling him but too afraid to advance.

'I have made you temporary gatekeeper to your son's oasis of his mind, where you will stay until I seem fit to return when I have decided on your punishment.'

'Are you are joking?' Stan said, feeling the strain.

Ictus ignored him, 'Your first duty as gatekeeper Stan, is to do me the honour of releasing my fallen angels Mono and Neutro. Then you can begin changing this desolate landscape by shaping it to something that can flourish and grow.'

'How and why should I do that for you?' Stan spat, feeling a strange sensation channeling through his very being.

'Because Stan, I would really like my angels returned to me as they once were and not in this controlled state that they are currently in. I also feel that you owe it to Nate to nurture his thoughts in time of need. What better way than to connect to your son from beyond the grave and be that voice in his head that looks out for him as you shape his unconscious world accordingly?'

Stan's head slumped, 'How do I do that?' he said defeatedly.

'The power of the mind is a wonderful thing, Stan; with it you can create anything you desire if you have the tools,' Ictus said cryptically.

Stan knew what he meant though, as he could feel the power returning to him. 'Let's just say I do as you request. What's to stop me from breaking my bonds?'

'That is out of your control, Stan. You see, the thing I put in the shallow of the pool below you, when we were here last, will grow in strength over the coming years, being fed by your thoughts and emotions until it is strong enough to take the mantle of gatekeeper from you,' Ictus said.

Twisting his head to see below him to the pool, Stan strained to see what was resting down there. 'So I'm a prisoner to you and this thing, then am I?' he said, failing to glimpse what it was down there.

'Yes, I suppose you are. But at least you have the

pleasure of looking after your son like a good father should. Doesn't that give you a sense of pride that you thought you'd never experience Stan?'

"So, what are you going to do now then, Ictus, while I serve my punishment here?' Stan replied, not wishing to give a direct answer.

'Your punishment? No Stan, this is not your punishment. That will come much later down the line, when I have decided something befitting for you,' Ictus replied, then added 'I am now going to return Mr Goole here to his own island, where he will go back to his life. Then I will recruit an army of good from the thousands of new souls that are on their way here as we speak, all gifted to me by the late William Last.'

The lost angels, Mono and Neutro, drifted aimlessly around as Ictus unfurled from its shielded state and rose up into the sky carrying the priest. 'Now if you'd be so kind Stan, release my angels.'

'Tell me one last thing before you go Ictus?' Stan said.

Ictus circled around, 'Go on.'

'Not all those souls coming to you will be innocent,' Stan said defiantly.

'No, they won't, but that does not matter, for those that are unworthy will be destroyed before evil comes to collect them, the rest will bow down and obey me.'

'You're no better than greedy men on Earth,' Stan said, straining his neck to look up at Ictus.

'But I am. You are all born then you die, the rest

in between is merely an illusion. I am the only one who deals in absolutes,' Ictus replied.

Stan watched Ictus with contempt as it took the priest and soared across the tree tops and disappeared from view, before turning back to the angels in front of him. He closed his eyes and concentrated his will into the very earth below, funneling his power though the tendrils and down into the pool. By the time he had opened his eyes, Mono and Neutro had become solid and returned whole.

'Thank you, Stan. May Ictus take pity on your soul,' Neutro said, before calling Mono to join her. They then beat their wings to the open sky, leaving Stan alone in solitary confinement.

*

Petra was curled up on her sofa at home sipping from her glass of water with her daughter Sally at her side, when her mobile phone rang. She set down the glass and snatched up the phone, immediately seeing Arlo's name displayed on the screen, 'My God Arlo, I've been so worried, where's Ana?' she said, putting the phone on loud speaker.

'It's me, mum. I'm fine honestly, I was in the middle of something when you rang, I'm afraid my phone is water damaged so that's why I'm using hubby's cell,' Ana answered to Petra's relief.

'What about your brother? Have you found him? Is he okay?' Petra said, flustered.

'All in good time mum. I need to know if you're okay? I know about Dustin... I'm so sorry,' Ana said.

'It's, it's not good Ana I'm afraid. It is definitely

my poor Dusty, but how do you know? Please tell me Nate had nothing to do with it?' Petra said, shakily bringing the glass to her lips to quench her dry mouth, wondering what Ana meant.

'I'm afraid it's not good news mum, is Sally with you?'

'Yes, she is dear. What do you mean it's not good, please tell me? Oh God!' Petra said, working herself up and looking uneasily at Sally.

'Mum, I will be home soon to explain everything. Can Sally hear?'

'Yes, dear she can, why?'

'Get her to turn on the television mum, it's important. Find the news channel and for God's sake whatever you do, don't drink the water. Look I've got to go, I'll see you both soon. Sally, look after mum,' Ana said.

'Of course, I will,' Sally said, putting an arm around Petra.

'But what about Nate?' Petra said, 'I need to know.'

'Later mum. I promise, it's madness here, I have to go now. I love you, bye, bye.' The phone went dead.

Sally turned on the television and found the news channel. She grabbed the remote and turned up the volume before rejoining her worried mum on the couch.

The anchor man wore a grave expression on his face, as he read the news aloud; 'Breaking news just in. An incident has occurred at the Mala Sort water treatment facility earlier today, where it has emerged that a contaminated body was discovered in the clear-well tank that supplies fresh water into the neighboring towns and villages. We advise everyone to please not drink water from your taps at this time until the authorities establish what the contamination is. In other news, an outbreak of a serious epidemic has claimed more lives, bringing the death toll to over two hundred so far. We will have more news as it happens. We just hope and pray that the two events are not related. Let's go to our correspondent at the water facility now...'

Petra looked at Sally in horror, spitting out a mouthful of water as the news became background noise.

*

Time passed slowly as Nate's oasis of his mind steadily changed from season to season and year to year, forever leaving behind the desolate traces of its former barren days behind. Stan, forced to shape the landscape, looked on helplessly as time went on without him, watching his son's life slowly blossom from afar by sense and feeling alone.

The pool of water below him too, had flourished and expanded, bringing with it a large pulsating cocoon that emerged from the water, as Stan looked on helpless, suspended from high above.

Stan watched the cocoon-like object stretch and contort as it outgrew the pool, leaving Stan feeling like he was a hen hatching an egg. It grew exponentially in size, stretching and contorting as the shadowy mass inside took on life.

Eventually, one day whilst Stan was just hanging around as usual, the cocoon hatched and spilled from its inners a familiar sight that flopped into the pool, getting Stan worked up into a joyful and elated mood.

Dustin had told him back when they first met that he had passed on Stan's old comic to his son Nate. Now everything became clear, 'Well I'll be damned. How the devil are you, old friend? It would seem that my son has the same imagination as me then,' Stan said, with a massive grin on his face, watching the figure unfurl its wings before him.

27

LOVING TRIBUTE

Some thirty odd years had passed since the atrocities had taken place. Tens of thousands of lives had been claimed and people still held vigils every anniversary to mourn the terrible loss of their relatives and loved ones.

Nathan Palmer, now in his forties, was promised that his treatment from his therapy had been very successful and was told by doctors that he would be ready to join society very soon, safe in the knowledge that he had no part in the genocide.

But although he had taken great strides in rehabilitation, nothing could have prepared him for the sad news on the recent loss of his mother Petra Palmer, who had just died of old age, well into her eighties. It had been lucky for her at the time that she only drank bottled water, so had not been one of the unfortunate souls that perished in the mass exodus for which no cure was ever found, with the Mala Sort water plant now laying defunct, empty and off limits, now just a grave reminder.

So here now was Nate, handcuffed in the back of a caged police van, dressed in a dark suit that his sister

Ana had given him that belonged to Arlo, with a dried daisy attached to the button hole on his lapel.

Sitting there outside the building of the Quietus independent funeral group, waiting for his sisters to arrive, Nate looked around nervously.

Sally arrived by car first, alone. She spotted Nate in the back of the van and quickly looked away as she locked her car and hurried into the chapel.

Nate became anxious and fondled in his pocket for a crumpled note, which he pulled out and smoothed out upon his lap, just as a roaring motorcycle came drawing up behind them with Arlo and Ana onboard.

The police officer, a blond-haired, strikingly beautiful female, who was in the front of the van, looked backwards through the mesh to Nate, 'You ready, Nathan?' she said.

Nathan nodded and waited as the officer exited the vehicle and then opened the rear doors. She grabbed a hold of his handcuffed hands and helped him to get out.

Ana removed her crash helmet and walked up to the young police officer, 'Would it be okay to hug my brother please?' she said. The police officer granted her permission and Ana gave Nate a big hug and a kiss on the cheek. 'How are you sweet brother? I gather it's not long now for your release?' she said, stepping aside so Arlo could come and shake his hand.

Nate released Arlo's hand and nodded curtly, 'Sally still wants nothing to do with me. The only people that visit me regularly are you guys. Do you think she will ever forgive me?' he said, catching sight of Sally through the window.

Ana straightened his daisy, 'Mum would have been proud of you Nate, I'm glad you're wearing her favourite flower that I sent you,' she said, slowly shaking her head. 'Sally wouldn't let me explain all that I knew back then, she said I was insane and that I should have been taken away with you. So, I guess we both have to live with her decision Nate. Shall I ask her if we can all go in to see mum together or would you like to go in alone?'

Holding up the note, Nate looked to the police officer, 'I know I'm not allowed to go in alone, but would you mind being in there with me? As I think it's best that I allow my sisters time together without me...' he said, then addressed Ana, '….if that's okay with you sis?'

"Of course, it is Nate. I'll let you know when you can go in then shall I?'

'Thanks Ana, yes I'd appreciate it,' Nate said, folding the note and slipping it back into his pocket.

Ana grabbed Arlo's hand and they made their way into the waiting room to join Sally, where they exchanged hugs and kisses.

Nate watched with sadness and envy as the three of them disappeared into the chapel and out of sight, wishing and hoping that things had been different. To this day he still had no recollection of the horrible deeds that he had apparently dealt to his stepdad, Blake and the water treatment guy.

By the time Ana, Arlo and Sally had finished viewing Petra in the chapel, rain had begun to batter against the large windows of the waiting room that

Nate and the police officer had taken shelter in.

Sally exited first and blanked Nate as she hurried passed and slipped out of the door in a flood of tears.

Arlo ushered Ana through the waiting room with a tissue held up to her nose and her head bowed low, he gave Nate a saddened look, 'Take care Nate, we will see you soon at the funeral,' he said, patting Nate's shoulder and steering Ana to the exterior door.

The chapel attendant saw the handcuffs around Nates wrists and kept one eye on him as he led them into the chapel, 'I will be right outside if you need anything,' he said, giving the police officer a wary look.

'Thank you,' Nate said, as he approached his mum's coffin and braced himself to look inside, as the officer slipped in behind him.

Tears of sadness flowed from his eyes as he gazed lovingly to his beautiful and frail old mum laying peacefully inside.

Her hair was grey, and her complexion was waxy, she was fitted out in a bright yellow summer dress with a brown belt around her middle and her finger nails were also painted yellow and were perfectly manicured. To compliment her look, she had yellow high heel shoes on.

'I'm sorry mum, for everything,' he said, leaning in and planting a kiss on her head. 'I'm happy that you forgave me, now I hope you can finally find dad and peace once more.'

Nate pulled the pressed, dried daisy from his

button hole and placed it in her closed palms. He looked around the coffin and saw a collection of photos that were placed inside. He picked up the photo of his mum and dad together and ran a finger across it, smiling at happier times.

Then he disturbed another photo, this time of Ana and Sally when they were young, he put it back and saw one hidden underneath of his mum and Dustin, he buried it again from the guilt he now felt. Finally, he spotted one photo that stood out more than the rest, it was of him as a baby being cradled in his dad's arms with his mum in the hospital bed, he figured Ana must have put it in there.

Nate pulled out the note from his pocket once more and placed it in the coffin on his mum's chest, swapping it for the photo of the three of them together, which he casually slipped into his pocket without the police officer noticing.

'Love you, mum,' he said, turning away, then to the officer 'Okay, I think I am ready to leave now. Thank you.'

28

PARADISE LOST

The sun was slowly setting on the horizon, creating a hazy shimmer as it slipped away below the line of sea level.

Ictus, the angel of death, sat hunched like a prehistoric bird, resting on a lonely outcrop of rock in the heart of the ocean, with Stan sitting crossed-legged by his side.

A fleet of rowing vessels were peppering the vast expanse of water ahead, carrying passengers toward their destination, the gateway born of the sun that was their portal to paradise.

'I take it you have freed me and brought me here for a reason then?' Stan said, watching the little boats bob up and down over the small waves.

'Yes Stan, I have.'

'So, you want to show me what could have been if I had followed you, the promise of eternal happiness.'

'If you mean the passage to paradise by boat with your loved ones, then yes, I suppose I do.'

Stan uncrossed his legs and brought his knees up to his chin listening to the waves breaking against the rock they were on, 'I admit it is very pretty here. I guess I never really had the time to appreciate it before.'

'If you look very closely at the boat nearest to us, then I'm sure you will recognise the occupants aboard.'

Shielding his eyes from the glow of the warm sun, Stan squinted at the boat that Ictus was referring to, 'Is that? Surely not. That's not Dustin is it? I often wondered what happened to him and of Heparin whilst I was watching over my son.'

'Look closer Stan, who is with him?' Ictus said pointing.

Standing up and walking to the edge of the jagged rock to get a better view, Stan immediately caught sight of the second person. 'No, it can't be. Screw you Ictus, that's not...' Stan said, as he leapt from the rock and started to swim for the boat.

Ictus reached down and touched the surface of the rock, that began to rise up from the sea, bringing Stan back onto dry land and causing him to flounder in the shallow water that then began to recede as the landmass rose.

Stan pulled himself up and started to try and outrun the ground coming up from beneath him, 'Not Petra. She is my wife, my soulmate!' Stan screamed, 'I won't let him take my wife with him to paradise!'

Ictus used his power to tilt the rising island towards him, sending Stan sliding backwards. He turned onto his back, carried by the momentum and slid back towards Ictus, 'Please Ictus, don't take my wife from me, I beg you!' Stan cried, as the island stopped rising and Stan came to rest back where he started.

'Petra was never your soulmate to begin with Stan. Look inside yourself and you will know this to be true. The time you had together had run its course, your love for one another had waivered. Love for a true soulmate is everlasting Stan, now let Petra have her happy ever after.'

Stan sat dripping wet on his knees crying, 'But I thought, we would work it out. Some things require commitment to get right Ictus.'

'That is why I am going to send you back. You will be reborn on earth and start over until you find your soulmate. Unlike William Last who tried to cheat his way to new life by possessing your son, you will never know what has come before, until you cross back here again. Hopefully under better circumstances.'

'So, this is to be my punishment then?' Stan said, watching the boats disappear into the light of the sun and drift away from view.

'Yes, but also your reward. Not many souls get a chance to start over. You see, you are all slithers of the same collective soul fragmented by time, until you all find one another and become whole once again. My position is to make sure that you all find your way back to paradise and not veer off to the other side, that is why I acted as I did. Just because war is seen from afar, it does not mean that it won't affect you. Life is but one large battle and we all must play our part.'

'Just like Nathaniel played his? You took away his chance of collecting his wife when she died by keeping him here, only to send her to paradise alone. In turn you made him a condemned man,' Stan said wringing out his tie.

'So, you knew about that then? Who told you?' Ictus said.

Stan removed his tie from his wrist and hung it back around his collar, 'I guessed. I could see the pain in his eyes. You should have committed me to the same fate that Nathaniel suffered, then I wouldn't have to experience this loss.'

'Don't fret Stan, your loss will soon be short lived,' Ictus replied.

Stan watched the last light from the sun vanish and the darkness blanket the sky above. 'What will happen to Heparin now?'

'Heparin will become your gatekeeper as Lysis has been reborn as your son's. I gather you had plenty of time to reacquaint with him?'

'Yes, I did. Thank you.'

Ictus stood up and stepped aside, leaving a pool of water beneath him. 'Your time has come, Stan. Step into the pool and be reborn.'

'So, this is my island, my new Oasis? When I'm born again, will I have free will?' Stan said, stepping into the pool.

'Depends on what you become next, you're assuming that you will become human again or even male. Who's to say, that is down to the luck of the draw.'

'Wait, what?' Stan said. But the ground had already fallen away and sent him back into the abyss toward home.

29

CODA

The curtains closed around Petra's coffin and the final piece of music played to its fitting end, signaling her passing. The congregation steadily rose to their feet and made their way out to the flower court at the rear of the building.

Nathan Palmer, again cuffed and accompanied by a police officer, watched them leave and then approached the curtain.

The moment he parted the curtains, a perfume scent from the Gerbera Daisy spray that adorned the top of the coffin, met his nostrils. Nate inhaled the sweet smell in and admired the orange and yellow display, recalling that coffin toppers were used to mask the decay of the deceased within the coffin. Shuddering, Nate cast the morbid thought aside and reached in with his bounded wrists, touching his mum's casket. 'Miss you mum, I hope my letter finds its way to you and brings us both closure,' he said, turning away and exiting the crematorium back through the main entrance.

Ana knew that Nate wouldn't be allowed to mingle with the rest of the family in the flower court, so she broke away and ran around to intercept him as he was led back across the carpark to the waiting police van. 'Nate, before you go, I would like you to meet someone,' she said out of breath, making him turn around to get his attention.

Nate stopped and saw a girl in her twenties step out from behind Ana, looking pregnant. 'This is my daughter, Daisy, that I have been telling you about, your niece. Daisy, this is your uncle Nate,' she said, deeply inhaling air.

Nate smiled, trying to hide his cuffed hands, 'Err, pleased to meet you Daisy, I see you look just like your mum.'

'Thank you,' she replied politely, catching a glimpse of his cuffs before looking away awkwardly.

Ana stepped closer to him and covered his bonds with her hands, whispering in his ear 'I think that she looks the spit of dad, every now and then I see his eyes and his smile. It's actually quite comforting,' she said, kissing him on the cheek, 'See you soon,' she added, turning away to join her daughter.

Nate watched them part and felt a strong sense of belonging that he had not felt for some time. His sister was right, it was like their dad was staring back at him through the eyes of Daisy.

Content, Nate went to turn away, when Daisy hurried back and threw her arms around him, 'Everything will be alright, you'll see,' she said, smiling at him and handing him a scan of her baby.

Nate smiled back, 'Thank you, I guess,' he answered, taking the photo and gazing at it, before slipping it in his pocket with the other photo. Daisy pulled away and began to walk off, leaving Nate standing there in shock, wondering what she meant by that statement, just as the officer came to retrieve him and lead him back to the parked van.

*

Petra's coffin was unloaded into the back room onto a wheeled lift, where it was then transferred into the incinerator.

As the coffin caught alight and the temperature inside rose, Nate's farewell letter to his mum caught fire, licking away at the writing scrawled upon it.

Dearest Mum,

In the years gone by that have corroded away my precious life, my only true solace has been music. I am allowed very little to sooth my troubled mind as I sit and await release from my confinement, save a stereo, the odd book, pen and writing paper with a framed comic of my dad's above my desk.

Each different genre of music that I have digested has evoked a stirring of emotions within me that relate to a certain time or place in my life. For my favourite genres, I have categorised them into hope, fear and life.

Whenever I think of dad, I play Gospel and it incites hope, hope that one day I will see him again as my memory of him has all but vanished. When I play heavy metal I think of you mum and it instills within me a fear, a fear of losing you and never seeing you again, the way you were, before I came screaming into your world and turned it upside down. For that I am deeply sorry.

Whenever I see Sally, Ana and Arlo, I feel the need to listen to soul, as they have shown me that life is for the living and you should seize every day like it is your last, even if you are abandoned and alone like I have felt most of the time. That's how soul makes me feel.

But recently, mum, I added a new category, love. This has taken a long time for me to find. A love for one's self and for the love of others. You may ask, what genre of music do I slot into that category? Love ballads would probably be your response, but no, to me it would be classical.

Why? You may ask, well the answer is simple mum. Most composers have the presence of what they refer to as a coda within their masterpieces, which is a structural element of a piece of music at the end of a longer piece of music, which is separate from the main part or structure. Basically, it's when you think the music has ended but then it starts again but with a new hook.

But what has this got to do with love? Well quite a lot actually, even when love for someone or something ends, another love comes to carry on from when you left off.

When I heard of your passing mum, your love for the world and the rest of us died with you, but only for you to carry it over to the other side in order to love again.

I will think of this when the music plays for you as the final curtain closes, knowing that deep in my heart, your love will rise up again when you depart this world to be reunited with those we have lost.

As difficult as a coda may sound, I feel that I can relate to it, being as difficult as saying goodbye, but hoping one day to see you again.

Forever in my heart

your loving son Nathan.

THE END

The books of the Oasis trilogy
THE OASIS OF HOPE
THE OASIS OF FEAR
by Matthew Newell are available on Amazon.

ABOUT THE AUTHOR

Matthew Newell was born and raised in the quaint historic town of Harwich, Essex where he currently resides with his family.

It had taken over 20 years to get his first book published and now with this his third and concluding part to the trilogy complete, he will spend some quality time with his family before deciding on his next adventure.